Since there was no way she could wrap up her confession in pretty words, she blurted it out. "I'm pregnant, Santo."

The silence that followed was unending, and deafening. Penny avoided looking at him. She didn't want to see the horror, the disbelief, the shock, the denial.

When he did finally speak there was recrimination in his voice. "It's impossible. You are mistaken." His accent was deep and there was nothing but harsh shadow across his face.

"No, I'm not," she declared, trying to keep her voice level. "I'm carrying your baby."

"But I've always taken precautions." Dark eyes were still disbelieving.

"Except once," she reminded him. "Naturally I won't deny you access to the baby, but—"

"The hell you won't!" Santo's roar rent the air and seemed to echo around them.

Penny's eyes flared a vivid blue. "Do you really think I'd let a man who spends more time at work than he does at home bring up my child? Not in your wildest dreams."

Her heart beat so fiercely that it hurt and, fearing that she had gone too far, Penny stood up with the intention of fleeing again, but Santo unceremoniously pushed her back down.

"We haven't finished."

"I don't think there's anything left to say."

"Marry me."

MARGARET MAYO is a hopeless romantic who loves writing and falls in love with every one of her heroes. It was never her ambition to become an author, although she always loved reading, even to the extent of reading comics out loud to her twin brother when she was eight years old.

She was born in Staffordshire, England, and has lived in the same part of the country ever since. She left school to become a secretary, taking a break to have her two children, Adrian and Tina. Once they were at school she started back to work and planned to further her career by becoming a bilingual secretary. Unfortunately she couldn't speak any languages other than her native English, so she began evening classes. It was at this time that she got the idea for a romantic short story—Margaret, and her mother before her, had always read Harlequin® romances, and to actually be writing one excited her beyond measure. She forgot the languages and now has more than seventy novels to her credit.

Before she became a successful author Margaret was extremely shy and found it difficult to talk to strangers. For research purposes she forced herself to speak to people from all walks of life and now says her shyness has gone—to a certain degree. She is still happier pouring her thoughts out on paper.

THE ITALIAN'S RUTHLESS BABY BARGAIN
MARGARET MAYO

~ THE ITALIAN'S BABY ~

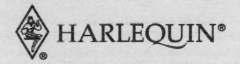

HARLEQUIN®

TORONTO • NEW YORK • LONDON
AMSTERDAM • PARIS • SYDNEY • HAMBURG
STOCKHOLM • ATHENS • TOKYO • MILAN • MADRID
PRAGUE • WARSAW • BUDAPEST • AUCKLAND

Recycling programs
for this product may
not exist in your area.

ISBN-13: 978-0-373-52759-5

THE ITALIAN'S RUTHLESS BABY BARGAIN

First North American Publication 2010.

Copyright © 2008 by Margaret Mayo.

www.eHarlequin.com

Printed in U.S.A.

THE ITALIAN'S RUTHLESS
BABY BARGAIN

CHAPTER ONE

FROM the first moment Penny looked into Santo De Luca's eyes she knew she was in trouble. They were the deepest, darkest brown she had ever seen, framed by long, silky lashes, set beneath a pair of equally silky black brows. And they appeared to be looking into her soul, trying to find out what sort of a person she was before she had even spoken.

It was impossible to ignore the rivers of sensation that flooded her veins, the way her blood ran hot, and the instant thought that she could be in danger. There was nothing to confirm this, just an impression, a feeling. The man was seriously sexy. 'Miss Keeling?'

Oh, hell, even his voice was sexy, coming from deep, deep down in his throat. Was there nothing about him that didn't set off alarm bells, that didn't stir her deepest emotions; emotions that she'd kept rigidly in check for a long, long time?

Penny nodded, feeling sure that if she dared to speak her voice would give her away. Never in her life had she felt such strong emotions at a first meeting, not when she didn't even know the man. Not when she was about to work for him. It was insane.

'You do have a tongue?' The voice had sharpened, still a low rumble in his throat but with an added edge, and his beautifully sculpted brows drew together over his eyes.

Such gorgeous eyes! Nevertheless his question had the desired effect. She snapped herself back into business mode. 'Yes, I'm Miss Keeling.' And she straightened her shoulders, standing that little bit taller. But even at five feet eight she still stood several inches below him.

'Do you look at all of your employers as though they're from a different planet?'

Penny wasn't sure whether he was joking or being serious. But just in case she kept her voice grave. 'Not as a rule, Mr De Luca.'

'So I'm the exception. Is there a reason for that?'

Not only did he look gorgeous but he also had a most attractive Italian accent. It raised goose bumps on her skin. And she wondered for a brief moment whether it would be advisable to work for a man who could do this much damage before she'd even got to know him. Perhaps she ought to turn and run?

'I… You're not what I expected.'

'I see,' he said. 'I'm not the normal run-of-the-mill father, is that it?'

Penny sucked in a deep breath. 'Normally it's the child's mother who organises a nanny, generally because she needs to go back to work—or whatever else it is she wants to do,' she couldn't help adding. She had worked for very rich women who preferred having a social life to bringing up their children.

'The agency didn't tell you that there wasn't a Mrs De Luca?'

'No.' She heard the surprise in her voice. Normally

she would have been given the background of the family
and they would have wanted to see her prior to engaging
her, making sure she was suitable. But on this occasion
a nanny had been needed urgently.

'You come highly recommended.' He raised a brow
as he said it, and Penny realised that she was hardly
being professional. In fact she was acting completely
out of character.

All because he was a strikingly handsome man.

'Though I'm beginning to have my doubts about
whether you're up to the job,' he added crisply. 'Nevertheless I have a very important business meeting that
I'm already late for. Come through to the kitchen and
I'll introduce you to my housekeeper. We'll have a
serious talk tonight.'

Up to the job! Penny took umbrage. 'Mr De Luca,'
she declared, standing at her full height, staring him full
in the face, 'I can assure you that I am more than up to
the job, as you put it.' She thrust an envelope into his
face. 'Here are my references, you'll see that—'

'Those aren't necessary!' he declared imperiously. 'I
prefer to make my own judgement.'

And at the moment she was sadly lacking, thought
Penny. She could hardly blame him; she had stood there
like an idiot instead of ignoring his sexuality and being
the truly experienced nanny that she was.

She had approached his house this morning with an
air of excitement. The agency she worked for had
stressed how important this job was. Mr De Luca was
the head of the De Luca advertising agency—a global
company—and if she pleased him it could work very
well for them.

He lived on the outskirts of London in a huge mansion set in an amazing estate—it couldn't be called anything less, she'd decided, because after the electronically controlled gates had opened she'd driven through acres of woodland and gardens. To say she was impressed would have been an understatement.

And when she'd reached the house, well, she was truly stunned. Three storeys high, eight windows across. How many rooms was that?

'I understand your last nanny left you rather unexpectedly?' she questioned as she hurried at his heels through miles of corridors. Anyone would think they were in a race. His long legs were in danger of taking him away from her.

He wore a dark grey suit and white shirt, both Savile Row if she wasn't mistaken, but they did little to disguise the well-maintained body beneath. This man seriously worked out and she wasn't surprised, he'd need to be super-fit to work the long hours he did. She'd been told he left by seven every morning, and was always late getting home. It sounded to her as though he didn't see very much of his daughter.

'That is correct. And if you're having any ideas that this job isn't for you, then I'd be obliged if you would say so right now.'

He stopped so abruptly that Penny cannoned into him, taken aback when his strong arms steadied her and those mesmerising dark eyes locked into hers. She actually stopped breathing for a few seconds and gazed into those magical depths, then realised what she was doing and stepped back a pace.

Her nostrils were invaded by the most irresistible cologne she had ever come across. It was strong like the man himself, though not overpowering. It was subtly pervasive and she knew it would linger long after he had gone. 'I will naturally do the job to the best of my ability. I'm a conscientious worker, your daughter will be perfectly safe with me and—where is she, by the way? Don't you think we ought to be—?'

'Chloe's still in bed,' he told her fiercely. 'I saw no reason to wake her. My office hours are irregular to say the least, but Chloe needs routine, as I'm sure you understand. Emily, my housekeeper, will show you around and then I shall expect you to get Chloe ready and take her to school. I didn't see any luggage when you arrived, you do know that I expect you to live in?'

Penny inclined her head. 'It was a rush getting here this early,' she said, hoping to make her point. 'I planned on sorting my things out while your daughter's at school.' According to the agency his previous nanny had walked out yesterday. Though why he couldn't have taken a day off and spent time interviewing, Penny didn't know. At least it was her gain, and the salary she'd been offered was far higher than anything she'd earned before.

He muttered something under his breath in his native language and then resumed his race to the kitchen.

Emily was small and rotund and Penny imagined her to be in her mid-fifties. She had rosy cheeks and short grey hair and, judging by the way she looked at her employer, she clearly adored him.

Penny didn't realise how much his presence filled the massive room until he had gone. It was only then that she felt able to breathe more easily. Emily saw her relax and smiled. 'Welcome to the De Luca household. Mr De Luca's a wonderful man to work for. I hope you'll be happy here.'

And why was the housekeeper giving her more of a welcome than the big man himself? wondered Penny. 'Is he always so disagreeable?' she enquired. 'I got the impression that he wasn't sure I'd be any good at the job!'

'That's because none of the nannies he's employed before have lasted more than a few weeks.'

Penny frowned. 'Is Chloe a difficult child? Or is Mr De Luca the problem?' He was actually a big problem as far as she was concerned. Far too sexy for her peace of mind. Penny had never met a man who so instantly affected her senses. Even Max hadn't had this sort of effect on her, and she'd thought he had been the one.

Emily lifted her shoulders and let them drop again, slowly. 'Mr De Luca's a very fair man to work for. I should know, I've been with him for a very long time. It's the hours that people don't like. Most of the nannies before were all young with fancy boyfriends and they didn't want to be on duty twenty-four hours a day. It's understandable.'

'Is that what he expects?' asked Penny, widening her eyes. No wonder he'd offered her such a good salary. He wanted blood.

'He doesn't think, that's his trouble,' declared Emily. 'You just have to tell him if he puts on you too much. I do.'

But she was part of the fixtures, thought Penny. He wouldn't take it very kindly if she said anything. She was tempted to ask what had happened to his wife but felt it was too soon. Perhaps she too had been unable to put up with the long hours he worked?

'What time does Chloe normally get up?' she asked, glancing at the clock on the wall.

'Half past seven,' answered Emily. 'She's a slow

waker. Believe me, you'll have your time cut out to get her to school on time. I'll take you up there now.'

Santo couldn't get Penny out of his mind — even in the middle of his important meeting. She was nothing like any of the other nannies he'd hired. For one thing she had more to say for herself—which could prove interesting! He wasn't averse to verbal sparring; he liked a spirited woman. It had surprised him, that was all.

She had long, wavy blonde hair which, if he wasn't mistaken, was entirely natural, the bluest of blue eyes surrounded by amazingly long lashes, a tiny retroussé nose and beautifully shaped lips.

He had also noticed that she wasn't exactly as slender as some young women aspired to be these days—stick-thin did nothing for him. She had curves in all the right places and even thinking about the way her breasts had jutted against the thin cotton of her blouse made his testosterone levels rise.

He surprised himself by recalling these details. Surprised and dismayed. He didn't want to think of her in this way. He could do without such distractions. He had enough on his mind already.

But he did think of her and he was disappointed when he got home that evening and she was nowhere around. He'd been looking forward to talking to her some more, finding out what made her tick, what her hopes and aspirations were.

He'd not even thought twice about any other nanny the agency had sent him, but Penny Keeling was different. She was, without a shadow of doubt, a very intriguing woman and he was looking forward to getting to know her better.

* * *

After Penny had taken Chloe to school she returned to the flat she shared with a friend and began packing her bags.

'You do realise I'll have to find someone else? I can't afford this place on my own,' said Louise.

Penny nodded.

'You seem very sure that this is the right job for you. It's happened before, you know, and you've—'

'I'm sure,' answered Penny firmly. Why wouldn't she be with such a high salary? It was every girl's dream.

'De Luca, you say, that wouldn't be the Santo De Luca who's forever in the news, would it?' wondered her friend. 'The one who always has a glamorous girl hanging on his arm?'

'The very same,' Penny agreed and smiled at Louise's expression.

'No wonder you took the job. I'd do the same in your position!'

Penny grinned. 'I'm not a man-hunter like you, Louise.'

'Life's too short not to enjoy it,' answered her friend with a shrug. 'You picked the wrong man once, but hey, who's to say you'd do it again? You've been on your own for far too long.'

'You're incorrigible,' laughed Penny, shaking her head. 'And I'm off. I'll see you soon.'

Now it was late evening and she sat in her own private sitting room. A room that was luxuriously furnished with antiques and brocade drapes and had floor-to-ceiling windows overlooking the parkland. It adjoined her bedroom, and the other side of her bedroom was Chloe's room.

Chloe was adorable. A bright five-year-old, a chatterbox, and she'd already told Penny that she liked her better than her other nannies.

When Penny heard Santo's car she imagined him coming in and throwing his jacket on the back of a chair, pouring himself a drink maybe. She imagined his strongly carved face, the high cheekbones, the straight nose and the slash of his mouth. Would his features be relaxed or would the trials of the day still be imposed on them?

Had he eaten? she wondered, and then laughed at herself for even thinking such a thing. What did she care? Emily had cooked a succulent roast of beef with all the trimmings and Penny had eaten every last morsel. Even Chloe had cleaned her plate.

In most of her other placements Penny had cooked for her charges; it made a change to have a meal provided for her. She didn't know yet whether this was the norm. And if so, what was she to do with herself while Chloe was at school? There were definitely a few things she needed to discuss with Mr De Luca.

He had said he would talk to her tonight. Should she go down—or did he appreciate solitude after a long day at the office? She realised that she knew nothing about him—except that he stirred her senses like mad.

On the other hand, they really did need to talk. Even as the thought flashed through her mind a loud rap came on the door, startling her, making her jump, sending her heart into panic mode.

'Miss Keeling!'

Oh, that voice. That deep glorious voice!

Nerve-ends tingled and a flood of warmth filled Penny's body and for a few seconds she could do nothing. She couldn't answer, she couldn't even get up. It was crazy feeling like this about a man whom she'd only just met, and more importantly a man she was now working for.

But how could she hide such vast emotions? Supposing they showed on her face? How embarrassing would that be? For heaven's sake, she was a professional not some giddy schoolgirl with a crush on her teacher.

She closed her eyes and took a deep, steadying breath, and when she opened them Santo was standing in front of her.

'Were you ignoring me, Miss Keeling?'

Not ignoring; trying to prepare herself for the onslaught of her senses that she knew would take place. And it did! With his shirtsleeves rolled up, revealing sinewy forearms and his top three buttons undone so that her eyes feasted on smooth, tanned skin, skin that tempted her fingers to touch, to feel, to taste even, she could hardly get her breath.

'I wouldn't dare, Mr De Luca,' she answered, surprised to hear how strong her voice sounded; no hint at all of her inner struggle.

Straight black brows rose and dark, dangerous eyes locked into hers.

He didn't believe her and she could hardly blame him. She felt like an idiot now and pushed herself swiftly to her feet. 'I was actually just thinking of coming down to see you. You said you needed to talk?'

'That is correct,' he answered brusquely. 'But we may as well do it here.'

Before she could even bat an eyelid he had taken the companion chair next to hers. The two armchairs in the room were overstuffed and not entirely comfortable and she almost smiled when she saw Santo's expression.

'How can you sit in a chair like this?' he asked, shifting his large frame. 'I'll get them changed immediately.'

Penny guessed that all the rooms in the house had been furnished by an interior designer with no thought for comfort, only aesthetic beauty. And they were beautiful chairs. But...

'Come, we'll talk downstairs. I can't sit here.'

He strode from the room and Penny had no choice but to follow. She devoured him with her eyes as she did so, noting the way his shirt stretched across his broad, muscular back, the way his trousers were similarly taut over his behind and hips, emphasising once again his athletic physique.

Was she crazy for noticing all these things about her new employer? Was she heading for danger? Ought she to get out while the going was good? Or could she be strong enough to hide her feelings?

They were so out of character. She had never, in the whole of her twenty-seven years, felt like this about a man she hardly knew. A man who—according to her friend—had a fierce reputation for eating females for supper. And he certainly wouldn't appreciate such feelings from his daughter's nanny.

He led her into what had to be his private sitting room, a fairly small room with lovely deep black leather armchairs and French windows opening out on to a patio area filled with tubs of begonias in every shade of apricot imaginable. To one side was a hedge of honeysuckle and the sweet scent of it filtered into the room.

Penny inhaled appreciatively as she sat down. 'What a beautiful smell.'

'I enjoy this time of night,' he agreed. 'Everywhere's so peaceful. Would you care for a drink?'

Much as she would like one Penny shook her head. She most definitely needed to keep it clear. It was intoxicated enough with the sheer sight of him. 'You have a beautiful daughter, Mr De Luca.'

He nodded and gave a faint smile. 'Thank you. How did you get on with her?' He stretched his long legs out, crossing them at the ankles, looking totally relaxed for a change.

'We hit it off straight away. She liked me, I think; I like her. You have nothing to fear. I will look after her well.'

'I'm glad to hear it. She means everything to me.' He picked up his drink, which he must have left on the table when he had come to seek her, and Penny couldn't help noticing what beautiful, long fingers he had, how well-manicured his nails were. And for a very brief second she wondered what it would feel like to be touched by those fingers, to have them stroke her skin.

Simply thinking about it created a storm and it took an extreme effort to dash the thought away. Fantasising about this man was a dangerous occupation. One she would do well to steer away from.

'I need you to tell me exactly what my responsibilities are,' she said, stiffening her spine and hoping she sounded efficient and businesslike. 'I expected to have to cook for Chloe but it would appear your housekeeper does that.'

'Emily does all the cooking and washing,' he agreed, 'and I have cleaners who come in on a weekly basis. Obviously I'll expect you to cook for my daughter when Emily has her day off. To be quite honest with you, Miss Keeling, I'm not entirely sure what a nanny's duties are. I—'

He pulled up short, deciding against whatever it was he'd been going to say. 'Naturally I wish you to take care of my daughter's welfare, but when she's at school your time is your own. Which in effect makes up for your early mornings and late evenings. Do you have a boyfriend? Will you be needing time off?'

'Needing it, Mr De Luca?' questioned Penny, her blue eyes sparking dramatically. 'It's my right. No one works seven days a week.' Her tone was sharper than she'd intended. Possibly because of the way her senses were still all over the place.

'So let's say your hours are flexible,' he agreed. 'And if you do have a boyfriend I must ask that you do not bring him back here.'

Penny looked at him boldly, her chin high. 'As a matter of fact there is no one. But surely that was something you should have queried before you took me on?'

He gave a very slight lift of his shoulders. 'I'm new to this game.'

'So you're making up the rules as you go along?' she asked.

Dark eyes narrowed and a muscle jerked dangerously in his jaw. 'Are you questioning my values?'

Penny drew in a swift breath. 'Not if my job depends on it. But I'm sure you see my point?'

To her surprise he threw his head back and laughed. '*Touché*, Penny. I may call you Penny?'

Oh, goodness, the way her name rolled off his tongue! He said it like no one else. Made it sound different and—dared she say it—incredibly sexy. Of course, he didn't mean it that way, it was his accent that did it, but heaven help her, the inference was there.

'Yes,' she agreed but she didn't look at him. She looked out through the open doors instead, where she could see a myriad of dramatic colours in the sky. The sun had disappeared but its aftermath was other-worldly. As was the situation she found herself in.

Santo's male hormones were behaving badly. And it annoyed him because he didn't want to be attracted to Penny. He'd had girlfriends, yes, in plenty, in the years he'd been alone after his wife had left him. But nothing serious. They all knew it was just a game to him.

But Penny was different. For one thing she was his employee—and it was a cardinal rule of his to never mix business with pleasure. And for another, he sensed that she wouldn't be into casual affairs. He couldn't quite weigh her up yet but he had the feeling that she wouldn't settle for anything less than a serious relationship. When she met the man of her dreams it would be an all-or-nothing affair.

And what a lucky man he would be. She had to be every man's dream. Beautiful, smart, capable, interesting. He could think of plenty of adjectives to describe her. Sexy, provocative... He stopped his thoughts right there and tossed the rest of his whisky down his throat.

Standing up, he said, 'It's warm in here, don't you think? Shall we continue our talk outside?' Where there was more air to breathe! Where he could put more space between them.

Penny smiled her consent and jumped to her feet. 'You have an incredible place here, Mr De Luca. I'd love to explore your gardens.'

'Santo. Please call me Santo,' he suggested softly.

'I'd rather not; it's a little too informal for our situation,' she answered swiftly.

He noticed that her eyes had turned from blue to amethyst in the changing evening light. They looked softer and more vulnerable—and, dammit, he didn't want to notice these things. She was here to work, nothing else, and he'd be as well to remember it. 'I can't have you calling me Mr De Luca when we're on our own.'

'How about Signor De Luca?' she asked cheekily, and he was taken again by the flash in her eyes. She was so beautiful, all woman, teasing and flirtatious, whether she knew it or not. He guessed she didn't; she would probably be horrified if she knew what he was thinking. How he was interpreting her behaviour.

'Tell me about yourself,' he said, conscious his voice was even gruffer than usual. 'I really know very little—except that you come with impeccable credentials, and that you have no boyfriend,' he added with a twist to his lips. 'Where do you live, for instance?'

'I share a flat with a friend in Notting Hill. Or at least I did, I moved out today.'

'I see. Would that be a female friend?' The question was out before he could stop it. Even though she'd said that she didn't have a boyfriend.

'Are you prying into my private life, Mr De Luca?'

He was startled by her question until he saw the twinkle in her eyes again and managed a smile himself. 'I'm very curious. Do you have any family? Of course you do not have to tell me if you don't want to. But I always take an interest in my employees' private lives; I always enquire about husbands or wives or partners, because if there's a problem at home it can sometimes affect their work and then I can make allowances. I believe my interest helps improve working relationships.'

She looked at him disbelievingly for a few seconds and then she laughed, and it was such a musical sound that he felt like laughing too. He wanted to pick her up and twirl her around. He wanted to kiss her; he wanted to… He stopped his thoughts right there, berating himself for being fanciful. And he was grateful when she spoke.

'In that case, if it will improve our relationship, the answer to your question about my flatmate is that she is female.' And she slanted him another glance to see how he would take it.

He pretended not to notice.

'Do I have family?' she went on. 'My father died when I was Chloe's age. And my mother died a couple of years ago; she'd been ill a long time. But I have a twin sister who has a six-year-old and a new baby. I visit her often. I love the kids.'

All the time she'd been speaking they had been walking along a flagstoncd path that led to the lake. It was a favourite place of his to sit and meditate—especially at this time of night. And he was looking forward to Penny's reaction.

It was not what he expected. When the vast expanse of water came into sight she gave a squeal of horror. 'Mr De Luca, you never told me about this. It's not exactly safe for Chloe. It really should be fenced.'

Never before could he remember feeling so deflated. And horrified. It had not occurred to him that it could be dangerous. He hoped none of the other nannies had ever let Chloe out to play on her own. He went hot and cold at the thought of what the consequences could have been.

'It will be done,' he declared. 'Immediately. *Mio Dio, sono un idiota.*'

'Otherwise,' said Penny, and he swore he could hear a hint of mischief in her voice, 'it's beautiful here.'

'It is especially beautiful at this time in the evening,' he answered. But he wasn't looking at the water, he was looking at Penny instead, and when she looked back at him with eyes so wide and so incredibly lovely he wanted to take her in his arms and kiss her—regardless of the consequences.

Penny saw the intent on Santo's face and knew that she had to act swiftly, or she too would give in to temptation. And how dangerous would that be? Her job would be gone and she'd never find another like it.

It had to be the incredible patterns of colour in the sky, reflected so perfectly in the water, that had done it. It was a place for lovers. It was a magical evening, everything still and hushed—and temptation was everywhere.

Not a place for an employer and employee. Unless she'd got it wrong and he hadn't been going to kiss her, but she couldn't be sure and she dared not take the risk. It would ruin everything, even though he was the most gorgeous man she'd ever met.

He wouldn't be after a serious relationship, just a bit of fun. And she wasn't up for that. She had many friends who would be—Louise, for instance. Friends who would tell her she was stupid not to go for it. Millionaires, billionaires, whatever, always lavished their girlfriends with expensive gifts. That way they didn't feel guilty when they dumped you.

Well, this girl wasn't for dumping. This girl wasn't going to enter into any kind of a relationship with him—except a purely professional one.

'Have you lived here very long?' she asked, deliberately moving a few feet away from him, pretending to watch a pair of ducks who'd broken the silence by squabbling on the other side of the lake.

He didn't answer her question. 'Why don't you have a boyfriend?' he said instead. 'A beautiful woman like you, I would have thought you'd have a whole string of them knocking at your door.'

Penny lifted her shoulders. 'I'm not interested in men. I'm a career girl.'

'You intend to be a nanny for the rest of your life?' he questioned, making it sound as though it was the worst thing she could possibly do.

'Why not?' she demanded.

'I cannot see it happening,' he declared dismissively. 'You're too beautiful to become an old maid. That is the right expression, is it not?'

Penny smiled and nodded. An old maid! It sounded so old-fashioned and not what she had expected from him.

'One day the right man will come along and you'll be swept off your feet. And before you know it you'll be married with a lot of little children of your own to look after. I'm sure that would be far more satisfying than looking after other people's children.'

'And you consider yourself an expert on that subject, do you? A man who needs a nanny to look after his own child.'

Penny saw him frown and knew she was out of order but for some reason the words wouldn't stop. He'd caught her on a raw nerve. She did want children; she'd thought once that she'd met the right man to give them to her. And ever since that disastrous affair she'd had doubts that there ever would be a Mr Right.

'Tell me, Mr De Luca, if we are being open and honest with each other, what happened to your wife? Did she leave you because of the long hours you work?'

The instant the words were out she regretted them. And when he spoke, when he answered her question,

she wanted to turn and run. She wanted to wave a magic
wand and make herself disappear. This was the worst
moment of her life.

CHAPTER TWO

'MY WIFE is dead,' Santo told Penny coldly. 'And for your information I have no intention of ever marrying again.' Without more ado he began walking back towards the house.

For a few seconds all Penny could do was stare after him. She saw shoulders that were hunched and a stride that was not his usual determined one. She felt like hell. What a stupid, inconsiderate question to have asked. What must he be thinking?

She really had overstepped the mark and wouldn't be surprised if he told her to pack her bags and go. And she didn't want to do that. She must make amends. Hurrying after him, she said, 'I'm sorry, I didn't know. I wouldn't have asked if—'

Abruptly he stopped and faced her. 'And you didn't think it would be wise to get your facts right before passing judgement?' His tone was harsher than she had ever heard it, dark eyes unfathomable. A tall, proud man, incensed at the way he had been spoken to.

Penny guessed he was still grieving. It must have been fairly recent. Maybe that was why he worked such long hours, why he didn't seem to be giving his daughter the love and attention that she needed. He wanted to blot everything out and the only way he could do it was to work himself into the ground.

'I'm sorry,' she said again, feeling her heart bounce in her chest, feeling a raw kind of pity for him. She wanted to hug him—how ridiculous was that? She wanted to tell him that time would heal. She knew how heartbroken she'd felt when her mother had died.

But he didn't want to hear those words. He wanted someone responsible to look after Chloe. He had a business to run, he couldn't look after her himself. He didn't know how. He'd never had to do it. He was the breadwinner. The man of the house. The provider.

'Forget it,' he growled, and headed back to the house.

Penny didn't follow this time. She waited a few minutes before retracing her steps and then ran swiftly up to her room.

She couldn't help wondering what Santo's wife had been like. There were no photographs anywhere, nothing to remind him of her. Was that deliberate? Was he the sort of man who couldn't cope with death? Pretended it didn't exist? So many questions with no answers.

When Penny got up the next morning, not surprisingly Santo had already gone to work. She'd not slept well with thoughts of the way she had upset him last night, and as she got Chloe ready for school she gave the girl an extra-big hug.

Chloe looked so much like her father, with jet-black hair and big brown eyes—which were sometimes sad. Penny knew that the little girl must be hurting deep down inside, bewildered as well, because how could you really explain to a child of her age that her mother would never be coming back?

It wasn't for her to say anything, though. If Chloe wanted to talk, fair enough, but she had no intention of bringing up the subject.

After dropping Chloe off at school she did some shopping and visited her sister before going back to De Luca Manor—as she had privately named Santo's house. It was hard to believe that one man lived in such a huge mansion. Why? Unless he entertained a lot, or had done when his wife was alive.

At the back of the house was a row of garages— she'd been allotted one for her tiny car—and Penny was surprised to see Santo's sleek black Aston Martin already parked there. He was home! At this time of day? She glanced at her watch. It was scarcely lunch time.

'Where have you been?' he growled the second she entered the house. It looked as though he'd been waiting for her. His black hair was ruffled and she could imagine those long fingers running impatiently through it.

'I'm sorry,' she said, jutting her chin, resenting the inference that she should have been in when he arrived home. 'I didn't realise I had to keep you informed of my movements. Actually I've been to see my sister. You did say my free time was during the day.'

'I thought I'd take you out to lunch.'

Penny couldn't hide her shock. 'Me? Why?' A nanny lunch with her boss? It was unheard-of, especially with a man such as Santo.

'Because we didn't finish our conversation last night,' he answered. 'But if you'd rather not, then…' He lifted his wide shoulders in a careless shrug.

'I'm sorry about last night; I—'

Santo cut her short. 'The subject's closed. Go and get rid of your bags. We're leaving in ten minutes.'

Meaning he didn't want to talk about his loss. And she could hardly blame him. People dealt with their grief differently. Santo clearly wanted to shut his away.

Penny scurried to her room. It didn't seem right lunching with him, but who was she to argue? She ran a comb through her hair but didn't bother to change. She was already wearing a long brown skirt and a pretty peasant blouse, both fairly new purchases and perfectly suitable. All she did was change her sandals to a pair of high heels and with a touch of lip gloss and a splash of perfume she was ready.

Was her heart racing because she had rushed? Penny wondered as she ran lightly down the curved flight of stairs towards Santo, standing in the huge hallway. Or was it racing because she was about to dine with him?

The hall below was elegant and beautiful with a polished wooden floor and a centre table holding a bowl of sweet-smelling roses cut straight from the garden. There was a rocking chair in one corner and ornately framed mirrors on two of the walls.

But at this very moment she saw none of it; she saw only Santo's unsmiling face. Unsmiling but indescribably handsome. She couldn't believe that she was actually going out with him. In all her years of being a nanny nothing like this had ever happened.

On the other hand she had never worked for anyone like Santo before. This was a man apart. And because he was different her heart was hammering so hard that it felt painful against her ribcage.

When the agency had asked if she'd take this job she had said yes without any qualms. What they hadn't told her was what Santo De Luca was like. They hadn't said he was one of the richest men in the country. They hadn't told her that he was gorgeous-looking. They had told her nothing. Maybe if they had she would have run a mile. Or she might have been so intrigued that she'd have taken the job anyway.

Santo watched Penny as she descended the stairs; he watched each step she took. He looked at the way she pointed her toes, he looked at her slender ankles, at the soft material of her skirt as it brushed against her thighs. His blood whistled through his veins. He watched the movement of her breasts beneath the flowered cotton top and his heart missed a couple of beats. Then he looked up and caught her eye.

She was smiling.

She looked as though she was happy to go out with him. Which both surprised and pleased him. Last night he had spoken harshly and regretted it immediately afterwards. She had caught him on the raw.

One day he might tell her that he and his wife had been divorced for almost four years, that any love he had ever felt for her had been killed long before then. And that Helena hadn't even told him that he had a daughter! If he'd known he'd have helped out, he'd have got to know his daughter, he wouldn't be in the helpless position he was in now.

His feelings when he'd discovered the truth were of sheer disbelief and outrage. He'd found it hard to accept that she had done such a thing to him. He'd never realised how much she had hated him. Even thinking about it, reliving that moment when he made his discovery, twisted his guts.

Thank goodness for Penny. Fiery and spirited without the least interest in him, which made a refreshing change. He was so used to women hanging on to his every word, fighting to make themselves noticed, trying to trick their way into his bed, that Penny was like a breath of fresh air.

No doubt she thought him an uncaring father, but the truth was he felt simply helpless. He didn't know the first thing about bringing up children. He'd had no contact with kids since he had been one himself. They were a mystery to him.

'Good,' he said, 'a woman who doesn't take hours to get ready. I'm impressed.'

'I haven't changed, I hope I'm all right. We're not going anywhere too posh, are we?'

She seemed faintly worried and Santo smiled reassuringly. 'You're not to worry about anything; you look incredible.' Had he really said that? He'd have to watch himself. This wasn't a date. She intrigued him and he was looking forward to finding out more about her but that was all. Even then she didn't have to tell him anything about herself if she didn't want to.

Except that he wanted to know!

He'd summoned his chauffeur while Penny was getting ready and he led her out to the waiting Bentley, smiling to himself as her eyes widened, well aware that his wealth impressed her.

She slipped into one side, he into the other, and they sank into the luxurious cream leather. The light floral scent of her perfume was evocative, teasing his nostrils like nothing else. And he knew that forever afterwards this particular perfume would always remind him of her.

Penny was on edge, her hands clasped firmly in her

lap, her knees and feet together, her back straight. She hadn't expected the limousine and the chauffeur or she definitely would have changed. This was very alien, and she prayed that he wasn't going to take her somewhere equally classy.

'Relax,' he growled softly in her ear, 'I won't bite, I promise.'

Penny edged away, unable to stop herself, missing his frown but aware that he didn't approve. It was that infinitesimal stiffening of his body that gave him away. He wasn't used to a woman moving away from him, rather the opposite. Part of Penny, a large part, didn't want to move away. Heaven help her, but she wanted to find out what it would feel like to be held against his hard, hot body, bound to him by arms of steel, but she knew where such pleasures could lead. She was entirely out of his league; he would use her and then discard her, the way Max had done. And she had no wish to go through that again.

Men didn't have the same sort of feelings that women had. Their emotions weren't involved when they embarked on affairs. They could walk away at the end without getting hurt. Not so for the female sex.

'Where are we going?' she asked, and was horrified to hear the husky throb in her voice.

'To one of my favourite bistros.'

A bistro. That wouldn't be so bad. Her breathing got easier. 'Why aren't you driving?'

He gave one of his twisted smiles where his mouth went up on one side and his eyes crinkled at the corners, making him look almost boyish. 'Because of parking. You know what London's like.'

'We could have taken the tube.' And then she laughed

at his shocked expression. 'I presume you never take the tube anywhere?'

'Not these days,' he admitted.

Not since he'd made his fortune, thought Penny. She could have made some comment about his carbon footprint but she didn't. 'Actually it's nice to be driven like this,' she declared instead, giving a little bounce on her seat.

'I noticed your car was pretty ancient,' he said, still with that half-smile.

Penny shrugged. 'Nannies' salaries don't lead to new cars. Though,' she added daringly, 'if I stay with you long enough I might be able to afford one.'

'I'll buy you one,' he said at once.

Penny's mouth fell open and she stared at him. He'd said it as though it meant nothing. Which it probably didn't. Not to him. But hell would freeze over before she'd let him do that.

'You look surprised.'

'As indeed I am,' she replied. 'Why would you want to do a thing like that? My car's perfectly reliable. I don't need another one just yet.'

'So you're rejecting my offer?'

He actually looked offended, thought Penny. 'I am, most definitely.'

'Some of the nannies I've employed have not owned a car,' he informed her, 'so there's one in the garage bought solely for the purpose of ferrying my daughter around. You're welcome to use it.'

'No thanks,' said Penny promptly, 'but you can buy my petrol, I'll let you do that.'

Dark brows slid up. 'A woman with morals. A refreshing change. I like it.'

Penny wished her heart wouldn't thump so loudly; she was afraid he might hear it. 'There are a few of us left,' she tossed smartly, flashing him a sideways glance.

If only he wasn't sitting so close! There was space between them, yes, several inches in fact, but not enough. She could feel the warmth of him even with the air-conditioning, and her senses were attuned in a way that alarmed her.

She was tempted to edge towards the door but didn't want to give herself away. All she had to do was remember that this was a business lunch. They were going to discuss exactly what he expected of her where his daughter was concerned. Just that. Nothing else. Not themselves, nothing personal.

So why was she worried?

'You're still not relaxed, Penny.'

She jerked her head round. He was watching her. Those incredible dark eyes were smiling and she knew that he had sensed her unease. More than that, he'd seen how rigid her body was, how her hands were still locked. She could hardly believe herself. She was behaving in a totally alien manner. Usually she was brimming with confidence, nothing ever fazed her.

Except this man.

Damn! What did he have that was different—apart from great wealth, of course? But that shouldn't have made her feel like a dithering wreck. What he did have, in spades, was sex appeal. And it was this that was troubling her.

She had never encountered anyone like Santo De Luca before. Plenty of men were good-looking, were good company, were great guys, were fun, and some even thought they were God's gift to women. But

Santo was like none of these, he was in a different class entirely.

At school she'd been in the drama group and, although she'd done no acting since, Penny knew that she would have to act now as she'd never done before. So she smiled, and she shrugged, and she said, 'It's unnerving having lunch with your employer after only one day. I feel like I'm under the spotlight, as though I'm going to be interrogated. Am I?'

'We'll talk about whatever you want to talk about,' he answered easily, his incredible eyes locking into hers.

To Penny's relief the car slowed to a halt. But her relief was short-lived when they entered the bistro. An informal restaurant was her idea of a bistro. Tables on the pavement, tables inside with checked tablecloths, candles in bottles with melted wax down their sides, everything nice and casual.

This was nothing like it.

To begin with it looked expensive, terribly expensive. The room was large, airy and formal. Tablecloths were white damask, the tables spaced well apart; there were fresh flowers on them and the silverware gleamed. You wouldn't get a bowl of fries here, that was for sure. Foie gras and caviare looked more in keeping. But she held her head high and pretended that she was used to walking into such stylish places.

If only! One meal here would probably cost a whole week's wages.

Santo was greeted with a warm handshake and respect, making it evident that he was a regular customer.

'This isn't what I expected,' she said after they had been shown to their table.

'It's not to your liking?' he asked immediately. 'We can go somewhere else if—'

'It's not that,' Penny cut in. 'I expected something a little less formal. I wouldn't actually call this a bistro.'

'To me it's a bistro,' he said easily. 'It's very relaxed here. And the food, it is *squisito*.' He circled his thumb and finger. 'You will like it, I promise you.'

Why are you doing this? she wanted to ask. Are you trying to impress me? She hoped he wasn't after something else. Fancying him was one thing but she would never allow herself to be compromised.

But she was worrying for nothing. Santo was a gentleman. He discussed the menu with her, passionately, and their food was perfect in every way. By the end of the meal she was totally relaxed.

They had talked about anything and everything except themselves. She did enquire which part of Italy he came from, which she discovered was Rome, but he had noticeably clammed up at that point. She didn't dare ask whether he had parents still alive, brothers or sisters, and she'd posed no further questions. Though she couldn't help but be intrigued.

On the other hand he had found out that her favourite colour was brown. 'Brown?' he'd asked incredulously. 'It cannot be your favourite. I can see you in something sky-blue or aquamarine, something to bring out the fantastic colour of your eyes. Have you ever tried those colours?'

Fantastic colour of her eyes! What else had he noticed about her? It was a scary thought. She didn't like the idea of her employer observing something so personal.

'Most of my wardrobe is in autumn colours,' she

admitted, 'and this—' she spread her hands, looking down at the skirt she wore, and her cream blouse with its tiny brown flowers '—is one of my favourite outfits.'

The moment the words were out Penny regretted them. Her blouse had a drawstring neckline and sat quite low on her shoulders, and she had drawn Santo's attention to it. She could feel his eyes on her breasts, which to her dismay hardened and tingled, and she couldn't help wondering how it would feel to have his fingers stroke them. The very thought set her senses sizzling and pulses pounding and it was with an effort that she dashed it away.

Surely it was time they went. She couldn't sit here thinking these thoughts any longer. She glanced at her watch. 'I mustn't be late picking up Chloe.'

'And I must get back to work. I've enjoyed your company, Penny. I feel I know you much better now. It will be a pleasure allowing you to look after my daughter.'

'You could always pick her up from school yourself,' suggested Penny cautiously. 'She'd like that.'

But Santo shook his head. 'I have another meeting at three. Edward will drive you home. I can walk from here.'

'And will you be home before Chloe goes to bed?' enquired Penny.

'I'm not sure. Probably not. Say goodnight to her for me.'

'Chloe hardly sees you,' she told him. 'It's really not fair on her, the hours you work. It would be nice if you tried to make more of an effort to see her.' Then she clapped a hand to her mouth. 'I'm sorry, I shouldn't have said that. It's none of my business.'

'You're damn right it's none of your business,' he responded fiercely, his brown eyes losing the softness that had lingered during their meal. 'I wouldn't be where I am today and Chloe wouldn't have the life she does if I didn't work the hours I do.'

But you no longer need to, thought Penny, though she wisely kept the words to herself.

Amazingly, though, he wasn't late home. Chloe was in bed admittedly, but it was only a little after eight and Penny was sitting outside with a book on her lap. It was a warm balmy evening and through the trees in the distance she could see the evening sun glinting on the lake and she couldn't stop counting her blessings that she had been given this job.

Many of her friends would have found the solitude boring. They liked people and music and parties, but she was not missing them. Not yet at any rate. Or was it perhaps something else that attracted her—perhaps it was the man of the house himself?

She was sworn off men, so why she felt this pull towards Santo she had no idea. She'd met plenty of good-looking men in the course of her work and had felt nothing for them. Only Santo had made her senses run wild.

For a few seconds she closed her eyes and pictured his face. She could see him as he'd sat across from her at the restaurant. Those amazing dark eyes that could fill a woman with excitement without a word being said. Even thinking about him sent a burning sensation through her lower body, made her head fall back and the tip of her tongue moisten suddenly dry lips. Oh, hell, she thought, was this really happening?

'Penny.'

The voice was soft—and close! She was imagining it!

Then a hand touched her shoulder.

It was real!

'Penny, are you all right?'

'Santo!' Her eyes snapped open and without even realising it she used his name for the first time. 'You startled me. I—I didn't hear you come in.'

'Evidently,' he said, his rich, deep voice throbbing through her veins.

It was the sexiest voice she had ever heard. And she couldn't help wondering what it would be like if he were whispering words of love. She felt sure that it could quite easily make her climax without him even touching her.

What a crazy situation.

'What were you thinking?'

'Nothing,' she answered quickly. 'You're home early.'

His mouth twisted wryly. 'I took your advice. I thought I'd see Chloe before she went to bed, but it looks as though I'm too late.'

'You've only missed her by about half an hour,' Penny informed him, struggling for composure. At least talking about his daughter gave her time to rationalise her breathing.

To her dismay he pulled a chair close to hers and sat down. 'Then it's just you and me.' He looked relaxed for a change, younger, less severe, and because of the way she'd been thinking earlier it made her want to—to what?

Touch her fingers to his cheek, explore the contours? See what it felt like to be kissed by a real man. Lord, this hadn't happened to her since Max. She'd deliberately built a defensive wall and now it was crumbling fast.

She couldn't do this, she mustn't allow herself to once more fall for the wrong man. Santo wouldn't be interested in her long-term. All he saw was a babysitter for his daughter, someone to take the weight off his shoulders. And if he could enjoy the pleasures of her body in the meantime—why not?

Now, where had those thoughts come from? He hadn't shown the slightest inclination to want to kiss her. But men were men. She knew that. Men took advantage of situations.

And her instincts proved correct when he leaned towards her, when his mouth was inches away from hers. She could see the pores in his skin, faintly smell cedar wood, and the whites of his eyes were so clear that—that she had to get away before she was lost in them.

Heavens! This wasn't really happening. It couldn't be. She'd only been here two days. He wouldn't pounce on her like that, surely? Risk the fact that he might send her running.

And she was right. He gave a satisfied smile and then sat back in his seat.

But she'd given herself away. She'd given him a hold over her. He knew that he could take her any time he wanted to.

'Excuse me, I think I'd better go and check on Chloe,' she said, jumping to her feet. She was gone in seconds, fleeing as fast as her legs would carry her, her heart pounding. Letting Santo see how she felt had been a big mistake. One he might take advantage of.

And she wasn't wrong.

She looked in on Chloe to find her sleeping like an angel, a faint smile on her lips, her black hair, so much like her father's, spread across the pillow. She was a sweet child and Penny couldn't see why Santo didn't devote more of his time to her, why he insisted on working long hours and getting someone else to look after his daughter.

Leaving the nursery, her head down, her mind still intent on what she saw as Chloe's misfortune, Penny bumped straight into Santo. The sudden contact whipped the breath from her body and though his arms steadied her she felt as if her legs were about to buckle.

'What's the hurry?' he asked, concern in his voice. 'Is Chloe all right?'

Penny nodded. Everything was all right except these dangerous feelings flooding her system. A response that rocked her. Ricocheted a hot sizzle of awareness through every bone in her body.

'Then it has to be you—or me—or both of us?' His dark eyes filled with amusement and before she could guess at his intent, before she could protest or even draw breath, he lowered his head and captured her softly parted lips.

Penny had always known that Santo's kisses would be sensational; nevertheless she wasn't prepared for the whirlpool of exquisite pleasure that wreaked havoc inside her. The way her world began to spin until she felt sure that she would fly out into orbit if he carried on.

For so many years she had told herself that no man would ever get through to her again—and yet it was happening.

Now! And she had no control over it.

Santo had reached into the deepest recesses of her mind and turned it around so that she was once again a woman with needs that required satisfying, fully and deeply.

When he pushed open a door and urged her inside Penny realised they were in his bedroom. One tiny part of her mind railed against what was happening, the other exalted in the crescendo of feelings that were tipping her over the edge into a world where nothing else mattered except this moment in time.

And instead of fighting him she gave herself up to the erotic sensation of Santo's kisses, breathing his name against his mouth, feeling the fire he had ignited take hold until it consumed her whole body. There was no room for questions, for wondering what was possessing her, all she wanted was to give in to the heated feelings that ravaged her senses.

Santo led her over to the bed, pulling her against him as they lay down, lifting one powerful leg over hers, tucking her head into his shoulder. It was a big bed, deep and comfortable, and Penny closed her eyes, forgetting where she was and what she was doing. All that mattered was Santo's hot body next to hers, the throb of their passion that must surely be loud in the room.

With gentle fingers he traced the contours of her face. The urgency of that first kiss had gone; he was exploring now, gentle kisses followed his fingertips, and Penny relaxed against him, giving herself up to the magic of the moment, urging her body ever closer against his.

He found her mouth again in a kiss that shattered her senses, made her writhe against him and call out his name. She clawed her fingers into his hair and felt such a surge of emotion that it scared her. She hardly knew this man and yet here she was in his bed, enjoying his kisses as though he was the only man in the world.

With all the strength she could muster Penny pushed Santo away. This mustn't happen; she couldn't let it. It was the worst form of insanity.

CHAPTER THREE

TREMBLING all over, her blue eyes wide and accusing, she scrambled off the bed and glared down at him. 'Is this why your other nannies left? You couldn't keep your hands off them?'

'*Mio Dio!* You really think that's what I am like?' Santo's eyes turned jet-black as he unfurled himself from the bed, and his silence as he moved towards her with all the lethal grace of a jungle cat was more menacing because of it.

'So tell me it's not true,' she challenged, finding it difficult to breathe. 'Tell me you were kissing me because you found me attractive, and not because I just happened to be available and you were feeling horny.' She stood her ground, glaring into his face, trying to ignore the sensations still skittling around inside her.

'I don't remember you fighting me off,' he returned coolly. 'It seemed to me that the desire was totally mutual.'

Damn him! He was right, but she wasn't going to admit it, not in a thousand years. And since he hadn't confessed to finding her attractive she had her answer. And now she felt stupid, and because she felt stupid it made her even angrier. 'Trust a man to try to worm his way out of a situation,' she muttered, heading to the door.

But within seconds a heavy hand had her spinning round to face him. 'No one accuses me like that and gets away with it.' Black eyes pinned her and the savage fury pouring out of them twisted her stomach into knots and stiffened every one of her limbs so that she couldn't move had she wanted to.

'Our desires *were* mutual and you cannot deny it,' he informed her icily. 'If it was a guilty conscience that attacked you, so be it, but never, I repeat *never*, accuse me of doing something I am not guilty of.'

'So this is the end of it?' Penny said, facing him boldly, her spine straight, her head slanting defiantly up towards his face. 'Or should I be on my guard? Is it likely to happen again?'

'That depends on you.' He let her go, standing a couple of feet away, but his body was rigid, his arms folded across his broad chest, and his fantastic eyes were fixed unblinkingly on hers.

A quiver ran through her. She was here to do a job, not enjoy an affair with the master of the house. He'd thought she was fair game and she'd almost succumbed.

She felt sick even thinking about it. 'If it depends on me then I can assure you, Mr De Luca, that this will never happen again.'

He inclined his head. 'So be it.'

'So be it,' she flung back and this time when she marched to the door he let her go.

Santo smiled to himself as Penny left the room. It hadn't surprised him that she'd put a stop to their passionate embrace. In fact he'd been surprised that she'd let him kiss her at all. There was no denying that he'd

enjoyed the experience. She was temptation personi-
fied. He even began to wonder whether it had been a
good idea employing her.

The other nannies had been stiff and starchy, and
Chloe had hated them so much that she'd been a little
minx. But his daughter apparently adored Penny and he
knew very well that life in the De Luca household
would be much more stable with her there. So—for the
moment—he'd have to curb his hunger.

IT WAS the middle of the night and Santo heard Chloe
calling for her mummy. She'd had these bad dreams
ever since her mother had died, although they had got
further and further apart and he'd thought she was
finally accepting the situation.

Being a father didn't come naturally to him. He
always felt awkward when comforting Chloe and had
never been able to find the right words. He guessed it
was because he'd had nothing to do with her early years.

Now he leapt out of bed, pulling on a robe as he
crossed the room, and in seconds was at his daughter's
door. To discover that Penny was already there. He
watched in silence for a few seconds, marvelling at how
good she was with Chloe, how her words of comfort
came pouring out as though she were a mother herself.

Suddenly Chloe spotted him. 'Daddy, I had a nasty
dream. Penny made me feel better.'

He walked across to the bed, glancing at Penny, re-
membering the kiss—how could he not when it had
made his male hormones run more rampantly that he
could ever remember? Resolutely closing his mind, he
turned his attention to his daughter. 'Then I'm glad that
I found her, *mio bello.*'

Chloe held out her arms to him and he immediately hugged her, conscious as he did so of Penny watching him closely. It was the first time she'd seen any physical contact between them and her faint smile confirmed her approval.

'Daddy, can Penny sleep with me?'

Faint hurt pulsed through Santo. Why Penny? Why not him? He knew the answer before he had posed it: because he hadn't yet earned his daughter's love.

He looked at Penny, felt his gut twist into knots, a deep need rising like the devil incarnate, and knew that he had to get out of here before he gave himself away. 'If Penny doesn't mind.'

Penny gave him a curious look before she smiled at Chloe. 'Just for a few minutes, sweetheart.'

'I'll see you both in the morning, then,' said Santo as he left the room, but he knew as he lay in bed that he was in danger of making a fool of himself where Penny Keeling was concerned. He wanted her as he'd never wanted any other woman in his life. Because she was different? He didn't know. Because he knew she would never chase after him as many other women had done? He guessed that was true. There was a special quality about Penny. She had integrity as well as beauty.

Whatever had made her succumb to his kiss, it wasn't her normal pattern of behaviour. He felt sure of that. Her body would be given only to a man she was deeply in love with. And the fact that she had almost given in to him had scared her to death.

The best thing he could do was distance himself from her. And his saviour was the project his company was working on, a global campaign for a major company that had always eluded them—and they were so close this time that he was prepared to work twenty-four-seven to make sure he got the contract.

Penny knew that letting Santo kiss her, allowing her emotions to surface, giving way to them, allowing him to see that she was not immune to his kisses, had been a dangerous thing to do. Dangerous and exciting. It proved that the hurt she'd felt when Max finished with her was finally being laid to rest.

Max had been a big businessman too who could have his pick of any woman he wanted—just like Santo. She'd met him at a party and when he had singled her out, told her she was special, she had fallen head over heels in love. Their affair had lasted six months and she'd been expecting him to ask her to marry him. The shock when she discovered he was seeing someone else had made her sick.

She'd actually been warned that he got through women like other people drank cups of tea, but he'd told her that she was different and she'd believed him. She'd been too swept off her feet by his amazing good looks to realise he had said this to all of his dates. Just like Santo.

When Max had dumped her and declared that it was all over she'd been devastated, while he hadn't even seemed to care. She'd decided there and then that she would never allow another man to get through to her. And until now it had never happened. Until Santo.

Perhaps Santo's Italian origins had a lot to do with the attraction she felt for him. She would love to find out about his family and why he was living here in England. He was different in so many ways, and he had that attractive accent to go with the voice—which did her no good at all. He had somehow wormed his way beneath the thick skin she'd grown—and how! All in a matter of two days!

She guessed that all he'd want was an affair. He and Max were too similar for it to be any other way. But even though Penny could draw comparisons between Santo and Max, she had to admit that the men were actually worlds apart. Santo was a prince compared to Max and, even though she knew she had to stay away, still she felt drawn to him.

Penny tried to ignore the fact that she had needs too, which Santo had awoken. She'd have to be very strong in the days and weeks ahead to resist her seductive employer.

'Where are Penny and Chloe?' It was the following afternoon and Santo had come home from work early, only to find the house virtually empty. He'd not been able to stop thinking about Penny, about the way she had responded to his kisses—and then abruptly withdrawn, blaming him! Nevertheless he'd been looking forward to seeing her.

'At a birthday party,' answered his housekeeper.

'Without telling me? She's taken Chloe out without my permission?' He knew he was overreacting, knew instinctively that Penny was trustworthy. But the thought of her bonding too much with his daughter gave him a feeling he didn't understand and didn't want to examine.

'I'm sure Chloe will be perfectly safe,' said Emily calmly. 'Penny's a nice girl and Chloe's very fond of her. They've really bonded—not like some of the other women you employed.' Emily sniffed her disapproval.

'I know, I know,' he agreed. 'Maybe they weren't the best choices. Even so Penny had no right—'

'You weren't here to ask,' reminded Emily in her usual forthright manner.

'So where is this party?' he wanted to know.

'At her sister's. It's her niece's birthday.'

'And you have the address?'

Emily nodded. 'Penny gave it to me—just in case. I have the phone number as well.'

'Penny, there's someone here for you.'

Penny looked at her sister and frowned. 'Who is it?'

'Chloe's father,' informed Abbie uncomfortably. 'And he looks anything but happy.'

Penny widened her eyes. Santo! Home from work early—once again! And wondering what she'd done with his daughter presumably.

'Don't you think you'd better go and—?'

Before Abbie could finish the tall, imposing figure of Santo De Luca appeared in the doorway. 'A minute, Penny, if you please.'

Penny looked at her sister then at Santo, and she frowned. 'I didn't expect you to finish work this early.'

'Clearly,' he said coldly. 'And you didn't think to ask whether I'd mind you spiriting my daughter away to a stranger's birthday party?'

'It's not a stranger's, it's my niece's,' she retorted. 'And this is my sister.'

Abbie lifted her eyebrows. 'Pleased to meet you, Mr De Luca,' but she didn't sound it and she quickly moved away into the kitchen.

'Whether it's your sister's house or not,' declared Santo, 'I would like to be told when you're taking my daughter anywhere new. I came home to spend time with her and what did I find? That you were nowhere to be found.'

To spend time with Chloe! Penny doubted that very much, and she was hurt that he didn't trust her. Her chin tilted defiantly. 'I didn't find out there was going to be a party until Abbie phoned this morning. It was a last-minute decision and I thought Chloe would enjoy it— she hardly plays with any children her own age.' Seeing him again caused an eruption of awareness. Her whole body became stingingly sensitive and she prayed her hardened breasts wouldn't push against the soft fabric of her T-shirt and give her away.

'You could have phoned me,' he answered. 'You have my number.'

'You made it very clear that I was to call for emergencies only,' she tossed back. 'I hardly call a birthday party an emergency.' Damn her heart for beating so loudly, for reminding her that she was in grave danger.

'Regardless, I wish to know your movements. I didn't know what to think when I got home.'

'I told Emily.'

'Yes, and thankfully she told me. And that's why I'm here. Where is Chloe?'

'You're going to take her home?' questioned Penny disbelievingly. 'She's having the time of her life. Why don't you join us?'

She said it tongue-in-cheek, knowing full well that Santo would run a mile from joining a kids' birthday party. Not giving away how much he had surprised her, Penny led the way through to the garden where seven children were running around shouting and laughing and enjoying themselves.

Chloe was in the midst of it. She looked happy and animated and Santo felt faintly guilty for storming in like this. She was safe! He should have known that; he should have trusted Penny. Hell, he did trust her. He was frustrated, that was what it was. He'd come home early, yes, to spend time with Chloe because Penny had made him feel guilty, but he'd wanted to see Penny too and she hadn't been there. His disappointment had been acute.

And now he'd charged in here and discovered everyone playing happily and he felt like an idiot. Not that he let it show. He stood and unsmilingly watched the children—until Chloe saw him and came running across, 'Daddy, come and play hide-and-seek with me.'

But Santo couldn't see himself playing hide-and-seek with a whole bunch of kids. He smiled, at the same time shaking his head. 'I've come to take you home, Chloe.'

Her face fell. 'Not yet, Daddy! I don't want to go. It's fun here.'

And she hadn't had much fun recently! Losing a mother was no fun at all. He sighed and gave in. 'OK, ten more minutes, but that's all.'

She ran off happily.

He turned and Penny was standing beside him. 'Thank you for that,' she said quietly. 'I've never seen Chloe this happy.'

'She misses her mother,' he acknowledged.

Penny nodded. 'There's no one who'll take her place. But you should learn to relax more with your daughter— you might be surprised how much fun you'll have.'

'I think I would have more fun with you, Penny,' he growled, his voice lowered so that no one else could hear.

Penny felt her cheeks grow warm and the blood raced through her veins so swiftly that she felt she might faint. 'I thought we'd sorted that out. Didn't you promise never to—?'

'I did,' he acknowledged rapidly and fiercely. 'But aren't promises made to be broken?' His voice had dropped to a low, sexy growl, for her ears only, sending more agonies swimming through her veins

Heaven help her, *yes*! But it would be fatal and foolhardy. Her body wanted him so much that it hurt, but she was thinking with her heart and not her head. There had to be a modicum of sanity in all of this. And letting herself be sucked into Santo's world of sensuality would be insane.

'Maybe in your eyes, but not in mine.' Penny dared to look directly at him then wished she hadn't when the full force of those dangerous dark eyes immobilised her.

'You can't deny that you feel something for me,' he announced softly. 'Even here, now, you're wishing that we were alone somewhere, that our bodies were joined, that you could—'

Penny clapped her hands to her ears and hoped no one was looking, or else they'd be wondering what her peculiar behaviour was all about. 'I refuse to listen, Santo. I made a mistake, one that I'm not likely to repeat. I'd like you to go, please, I'll bring Chloe home in a little while.'

She felt as though her insides were unravelling, that soon she'd be no more than a heap of bones at his feet. She couldn't take any more of this. It was unreal. She caught her sister's eye and mouthed the word 'help'. Abbie immediately came across the lawn to them. 'Santo, I'd just like to say what a lovely daughter you have. She's a credit to you.'

Santo puffed up like any other proud parent and smiled warmly at Abbie. 'Well, thank you—er—Abbie, isn't it? Actually it's more credit to her mother than to me, but, yes, she's a good girl.'

'And I'm sure Penny's a marvellous help to you. She's wonderful with children. She's always said she'd like at least three of her own.'

'Abbie!' said a startled Chloe.

'Well it's true, isn't it?'

'Yes, but it's not for everyone's ears. Especially my boss's. What must he be thinking?'

'I'm thinking, Miss Penny Keeling,' said Santo with a warm smile that did things to her that should never be allowed, 'that there's a lot about you I don't know, and it will be my pleasure to find out.'

Penny glanced from Santo to her sister—saw the way Abbie's brows rose questioningly, and knew she'd soon be interrogated. Abbie had always said it was time she found herself another man and she might be thinking that Santo was an ideal candidate.

'I think not, Mr De Luca,' she declared. 'I'd prefer our relationship to remain purely professional.'

An eyebrow rose, dark eyes condemned. 'In that capacity then I insist you bring Chloe home immediately.'

'You can't do that,' she protested, anger rising inside her. 'She's enjoying herself. Surely you can see that?' They both looked across at where Chloe was peeping out from behind a bush, squealing and darting out of sight again when one of the others spotted her. 'She's having a wonderful time,' insisted Penny. 'What's she going to do at home with only adults for company?'

'I said ten minutes and those ten minutes are up,' he answered, his eyes clashing with hers. 'Chloe!' He called her name loudly and his daughter came running. 'We're going now,' he said, his voice more gentle.

Chloe looked across at Penny. 'Do I have to?' And she looked as though she wanted to burst into tears.

Penny couldn't go against her father's wishes, not in front of the girl anyway, so she reluctantly nodded, her heart aching when she saw Chloe's lower lip tremble.

When Penny looked at her sister she saw that Abbie also thought Santo was being too hard on Chloe. Was it her fault for daring to speak to him the way she had? The trouble was she was scared of the feelings he managed to arouse and biting back was her only defence.

'Are you coming too?' he asked Penny, causing her head to jerk back in his direction.

'If it's all right with you I'll stay and help my sister,' she said, 'but I'll be home in time to put Chloe to bed, you can be sure of that.'

Santo's eyes narrowed but he said nothing, walking away with Chloe's hand held tightly in his. The girl looked back over her shoulder and Penny smiled. 'I'll see you soon,' she whispered.

'He's a swine, isn't he?' questioned Abbie as soon as he was out of earshot. 'I know he's a killer in a business sense, and he's damn sexy-looking, but he hasn't got a clue when it comes to his own daughter.'

'I don't think he even knows what he's done,' sighed Penny. 'It's me he's angry with and I expect I shall hear about it when I get back.'

'But you can't be expected to answer to him all of the time. He's put you in charge of his daughter and as such you should be allowed to make decisions. His attitude stinks if you ask me.'

Penny didn't want to run him down so she said nothing. She had a secure, well-paid job now and didn't want to jeopardise it. Part of her knew that there was more to Santo's sudden arrival at the party and that it was a purely private part of his life. Besides Abbie had a habit of repeating conversations to her friends.

By the time all the children had gone home and Penny had helped Abbie tidy up, it was nearly seven o'clock. Santo was waiting for her when she got home. He'd changed into a pair of casual linen trousers teamed with a half-sleeved shirt. He looked gorgeous and Penny couldn't stop her blood warming up and pulsing rapidly through her veins.

'I'd begun to think you weren't coming,' he said, his voice rich and sexy, arousing her in an instant.

'I'd never let Chloe down,' she answered evenly, 'but if I might be permitted to say, I thought you were wrong in taking her away from the party. She was enjoying herself so much. It wasn't fair on her or her hostess.'

'Your sister complained?' he asked sharply.

'Of course not!' she declared. 'But it wasn't good manners. It wasn't as though you had a valid excuse. Top and bottom of it was that you didn't feel comfortable.'

'And you're an expert on my feelings?' he asked scathingly.

How she wished that she were. Not the sort of feelings he was talking about, but sensual feelings, ones that sent the body into spasm and demanded fulfilment.

The sort that she felt at this very moment!

'I wouldn't dare to be so presumptive,' she told him tightly. 'If you'll excuse me I'll go up to Chloe. Is she in her playroom?' On the top floor of the house he'd had a room decorated especially for Chloe to play in. It was a child's delight with every sort of toy imaginable. But she wasn't old enough to play for long periods on her own and in Penny's opinion it was a sheer waste of money.

'No, she's in bed.'

Penny looked at Santo in surprise. 'You put her to bed?' He nodded.

'And she's asleep?' She could hardly believe what she was hearing. But at least it was a step in the right direction so maybe he was heeding her words after all.

'I think so.'

Penny wanted to find out for herself and took the stairs quickly, half expecting him to call her back, relieved when he didn't.

She popped her head into Chloe's room, saw that she lay very still, and was about to leave when the girl's tiny voice called out to her. 'Penny.'

Swiftly she crossed to the bed. 'What is it, sweetheart?'

'Daddy doesn't love me.'

Her words struck a chill in Penny's heart. 'I'm sure he does, darling. What makes you say that?'

'He wouldn't let me stay at the party. And I wanted to wait up for you but he said I had to go to sleep. He doesn't love me like Mummy did. I miss my mummy. She'd have kissed me and held me until I went to sleep.' And she broke down in tears.

Penny lay down on the edge of the bed and cuddled Chloe against her, dabbing her eyes with a tissue. 'I'm sure your daddy loves you very much, darling, and he doesn't mean to be mean to you. He needs help from you, as well, you know. Don't forget he must be hurting too. He loved your mummy just as much as you did.'

'So why didn't he live with us?' asked Chloe, her eyes wide and questioning. 'I didn't know I had a daddy until he came for me when Mummy died.'

CHAPTER FOUR

PENNY felt as though all the breath had been knocked out of her body. She could hardly breathe. She had presumed Santo and his wife had still been living together when she died. Not that they were separated, maybe even divorced. She wished he had told her, it explained a lot.

Even so, it didn't account for the fact that he had never visited his daughter. Why had he ignored her, pretended that she didn't exist? Supposedly he'd had no feelings left for his wife, but his offspring, his own flesh and blood, his little girl, how could he have failed her like this? Chloe's psyche might be harmed forever more.

The man was obviously a callous, uncaring, insensitive swine, and she was going to tell him so. As she charged down the stairs in search of Santo Penny barely held on to her temper. But she couldn't find him.

She banged open doors, looking into each room in turn, finally finding him in his study, feet up on the desk, looking totally relaxed until she burst in. The surprise on his face would have made her laugh at any other time, but not today, not now. She was ready for battle.

He unfolded his legs and stood up. 'Is something

wrong?' He stood at his tallest and proudest, his initial smile of welcome fading abruptly, replaced by a frown.

Penny skidded to a halt. 'You can bet there is, Mr De Luca.' She drew in several steadying breaths, choosing her words carefully. 'Chloe's just told me something that's shocked me to the core.'

'Chloe?' His eyes widened in surprise. 'I thought she was asleep.'

'Then I guess she was pretending,' she flared. 'Thinking about it, though, it's hard to imagine how she could sleep when she feels her father never shows her any love!' Penny glared at him, angry on behalf of the little girl who only wanted his love. 'If Chloe didn't need me I'd walk out of here right now.'

Santo folded his arms, his eyes dangerously dark as he looked down the length of his nose. 'I'd be careful if I were you, Miss Keeling. You're overstepping the mark.'

'I don't care,' she riposted, even though the blaze in his eyes sent a faint shiver of fear through each of her limbs.

When Santo took a step towards her she stood her ground, blue eyes clashing with brown, all senses on full alert. She sucked in a deep breath, then wished she hadn't when he stood so close to her she could almost taste him. His cologne invaded her nostrils, reminded her that— No! *No!* She must not go down that road.

Move away, she yelled silently. Don't come near me!

But she remained where she was, not letting her eyes waver from his for one second.

'So, tell me what Chloe has said to make you so angry.' His accent had thickened, he was very much the Italian— volatile, proud, ready to defend himself to the core.

As far as Penny was concerned he had no defence. Abandoning his child was simply inexcusable.

She allowed herself the pleasure of staring into his eyes for a few seconds more, ignoring the wild beating of her heart, the rushing of blood through her veins. She was so angry she could have pummelled her fists against his hard chest and declared him the vilest man on earth.

'Tell me why,' she said in her coldest, most disapproving voice, 'why you never...' Then she stopped. 'No, something else first. Why did you give me the impression that you and your wife were still living together when she died?'

Her question clearly took him by surprise. His head went back, his eyes narrowed dangerously. 'Did I? I don't think I *ever* implied that, Penny. In any case my private life is no concern of yours—you work for me!' And he stood even taller, a cold gleam of disapproval filling his eyes, making them icier and more condemning than before.

'You've put me in charge of your daughter,' she declared strongly, 'and, as she's upset, it's my duty to try and put matters right.'

'Chloe's upset?' The news jolted him, his frown now one of a very different nature. Questioning, not condemning. Even concerned.

Which Penny didn't believe for one second, not after what Chloe had told her. Kids didn't lie, not five-year-olds anyway; they said exactly what was on their minds.

'I think she has every right to be when she believes that her father doesn't love her.'

'She said that?' He almost choked on the words.

Penny nodded, a little of her anger subsiding at his shocked reaction.

'And you believed her?'

'It doesn't matter what I believe—it's what Chloe believes. And why wouldn't she when you never went to see her once from the day she was born to the day her mother died?' Penny glared, daring him to deny it.

'You have no idea what you're talking about,' he snarled.

Penny watched the way muscles tensed in Santo's jaw, the way his fingers curled into fists, the way his body grew tenser, and she sucked in a deep breath. She'd better watch out. Goading him any further could end in disaster. He looked as though he was about to launch himself at her.

'Then tell me,' she demanded. 'Tell me exactly why Chloe believes such a thing and why she herself told me she didn't even know about you until her mother died.'

Suddenly something happened to his eyes. Anger was replaced by blankness, as though he was not looking at her at all, as though he was looking back into the past—and the memories were not happy ones.

Naturally. He had a conscience bigger than the Empire State Building!

It seemed like minutes before he answered, and when he spoke it was so quietly that she strained to hear.

'Because my wife never told me I had a daughter.'

There was such raw hurt in his eyes now, in his voice, that it took Penny's breath away.

'She was pregnant when she left me but I had no idea. She moved away. The divorce was settled through our respective lawyers. I had no more contact with her. Keeping Chloe from me was her last selfish act.'

Penny stood stock-still, lost for words. How could any woman deny her husband, or ex-husband for that matter, knowledge of his child? How could she? And now her heart went out to Santo. She was deeply sorry that she'd spoken to him the way she had. She felt as guilty as hell.

'I didn't know,' she declared huskily.

'How could you?'

'I'm sorry. I know it doesn't help, but I am. Truly.' And without even thinking she went to him, not quite touching but almost, lifting her face to look up into his pain-filled eyes. 'Truly.'

With a groan he pulled her hard against him. Penny dropped her head back, still looking into those deeply troubled eyes, and when his head bowed down to hers, when he took her mouth in a kiss that was both savage and furious, she knew that this was his way of ridding his mind of painful thoughts.

And because it was what she wanted too, because the coming together of their bodies had set off a riot of sensation, she returned his kiss, feeling it drugging her senses, filling her with an overwhelming desire to be made love to. And almost as though he'd read her thoughts Santo growled in her ear, 'Penny, sleep with me tonight.'

Penny knew that it wasn't because of any mistaken feelings of love. It was because he wanted to blot out everything that he'd told her. He could have got drunk, of course, that was one way of doing it. But instead he wanted to lose himself in her body, and heaven help her, she wanted him too.

Crazy, ridiculous, when she was dead set against getting involved with any man again. But this wouldn't be a true involvement. This would be a one-off, she would make sure of that. It couldn't do any harm, could it?

All these thoughts and more whizzed through her brain at the same time as she answered his question with a kiss so passionate that she couldn't believe this was really her. She had never done anything so dangerously impulsive in her life. And the odd thing was, she didn't even stop to wonder whether she would regret it.

Santo groaned deep in his throat and the next second she was swung up by a pair of strong arms, held against a hard, hot, throbbing body and carried upstairs as though she were no heavier than his daughter.

Penny felt his heart pounding against her, and the scent of his skin was almost suffocating. He was more male than any other man she knew, drugging her with his nearness, with the awareness of his arousal. It invoked an equal intensity in herself, in her needs, in her hunger to be satiated by this man.

Right from the very beginning she had felt drawn to him. Santo was the sort of man who could not be ignored. By anyone. Sexuality poured from him. No woman in her right mind would turn him down. And she was no different.

She needed him. Desperately. And she arched her back, lifting her head so that he could kiss her again. The kiss aroused, stirred emotions; sent excitement slithering through sensitised nerve-ends so that his lightest touch increased her need.

Penny wasn't sure what she expected when they reached his bedroom. Would he throw her down on the bed and take her immediately? Would it be swift and furious before he thanked her and let her go? Or would he take his time, lose himself slowly in her body, determinedly shut out all unhappy memories; insist she stay with him the whole night through?

As the door closed quietly behind them Santo relaxed his arms and she fully expected him to let her go. But instead he slid her deliberately and unhurriedly down the length of his hard, hot body—inch by excruciating inch, ensuring she knew exactly how much he wanted her.

His arousal was magnificent, it couldn't be ignored. The fierceness of it drugged her, excited her, made her own need so deep and painful and mindless that she pressed herself urgently against him, her arms linking around his neck, pulling his head down to meet her parted lips.

It was a fierce kiss, an erotic kiss, his tongue invading, touching, stroking, inciting. Triggering an even wilder response. Penny clutched at his head, lacing her fingers through his strong black hair, feeling herself being swept into a place she'd never been before, a place where nothing mattered except Santo.

The touch of his mouth on hers, the taste of his kisses, the masculine scent of him. Strong. So strong it was more intoxicating than alcohol.

Actually she felt drunk. Drunk with desire. A deep real need screamed through her body with the force of a cyclone. She felt compelled to cling to Santo in case she got blown away.

How it happened Penny didn't quite know, but one moment they were standing just inside his bedroom, kissing. More than kissing. They were practically devouring one another. And the next they were lying on his bed and all her clothes had been removed.

Santo's too. His long, hard, exciting body lay next to hers. Olive skin against milky pale. An exciting combination. His torso was well-honed, as were his legs.

She looked delicate beside him. Not that she wasn't fit, but against Santo she looked like a china doll.

His darkly mesmerising eyes locked into hers as long, sure fingers began an exploration that threatened to explode her senses. Penny had expected that he would take her urgently and masterfully without any preliminaries. How wrong she was. Fingertips traced and memorised each curve of her cheeks, her ever-so-slightly upturned nose, the fine shape of her eyebrows, the delicate curl of her ears.

When he reached her lips she was screaming with silent need and sucked his fingers hungrily into her mouth, touching his face too, discovering hard lines and jutting angles. A proud man, a fantastically handsome man. Arrogant, yes. Masterful, yes. But at this moment completely dependent on her.

He needed her. He wanted her to obliterate his unhappy thoughts. He wanted to lose himself in her, beside her, with her. And she was happy to oblige.

Somewhere deep down in Santo's mind was the knowledge that he was doing a very dangerous thing. He didn't want a relationship. He had no intention of getting involved with his daughter's nanny. What he did need was release from the torment in his soul.

It had almost crucified him to hear that his own daughter believed he didn't love her. And tomorrow he intended doing something about it. But for now he needed to immerse himself in a distraction of a very different kind. And so long as Penny knew how he felt, so long as she didn't expect something more from him, then it was the perfect antidote.

'You do know what you're doing?' he asked thickly against her mouth, his breathing deep and hungry.

Drinking from her lips was like tasting the most exquisite wine, it was an aphrodisiac, making him want more, and then more again. In that instant he knew that this was not going to be a one-off.

It was more than dangerous. It was suicidal. Perhaps he ought to back out now while there was time? But already Penny was whispering her response. 'I know, Santo, and I can't help myself. I want you too.'

He sucked in a deep breath of air, feeling the taste of her on his lips. Feeling her supple body against his. Tantalising, beckoning, threatening. With a rough groan he claimed her mouth in another hot, reckless kiss that began the process of easing his pain.

Penny felt the sudden change in him, as though he'd freed himself of any doubts. And because he felt free, she did too. She abandoned herself to his kisses, returned them fiercely and hungrily, and when he left her mouth to explore the curve of her jaw and the slender column of her throat her head fell back against the pillow, her fingers returning to the wiry strength of his hair, clutching at the dark threads, accustoming herself to the shape of him, the feel of him.

But when his mouth moved even lower, when both his lips and fingertips found her breasts, discovered the hard nub that both protested and exalted when he teased it between thumb and forefinger, her hands flopped to her sides, her breath coming out in short gasps.

'Oh, Santo.'

At the sound of her voice he paused and lifted his head. His dark eyes were glazed and she wasn't even sure that he was focusing on her. 'You don't like it?'

'Like it? I love it!'

It was all he needed. He groaned and returned his attention to first one breast and then the other, suckling, biting, kissing, stroking, making her body arch with excitement, needing more—much, much more. Had she really said those words out loud? She sucked in deep breaths of air and closed her eyes to everything except the sheer exquisite pleasure of the moment.

Santo was an expert when it came to lovemaking. He knew exactly what would whip her body into a frenzy, what would make her curve herself into him, touch him too, run her fingers over his firm, warm skin, feel the strength of muscle, even the aching need deep down inside him.

When his mouth trailed a blazing line of kisses from her breasts to her navel, when his tongue explored, when she felt her skin prepare to ignite, when his fingers began to explore even lower, seeking the hot, moist heart of her, Penny could hardly breathe.

Her head moved from side to side on the pillow and she closed her eyes, conscious of nothing except this feeling of Santo being in charge of her body, instructing it to obey his commands, to burst into flames at a touch, to feel an explosion of sensation that she'd never felt before. Never!

It couldn't be the real Penny Keeling who was experiencing this serious metamorphosis. Things like this didn't happen to her. She was either dreaming or imagining it.

The Penny Keeling she knew would never have allowed herself to get into this situation. She didn't approve of affairs. One failed relationship had been enough. She was sensible, level-headed, careful...

Who was she trying to kid? Santo De Luca had somehow—she couldn't figure out how—deluded her into believing that she wanted him to make love to her, that it would be OK to give in to temptation.

And she didn't have the strength to rail against it. She'd known what she was getting into from the very start. She wanted Santo to make love to her. Now! This very minute. Deeply and furiously, assuaging the need that had built up and built up so that if he didn't take her soon she would turn the tables and climb on top of him.

'You're ready?'

Had Santo read her mind?

Penny nodded, then realised he wasn't looking at her face—he was too busy exploring other interesting areas of her anatomy. 'Yes.' It was more a squeak than a proper word but she arched her hips upwards and Santo groaned.

He moved away for the briefest of seconds while he sheathed himself and then he was inside her. So gently at first, so carefully, until he felt her fully relax—or was it when her hands clenched on his shoulders and she urged herself closer, repositioning her body, making it easier for him?

What happened afterwards was a blur of serious sensations, of nails digging into skin, of bodies bucking and gyrating, of primitive sounds escaping both their throats, of a final explosion that rocked and pulsated, bathing them both in a sheen of sweat, pounding hearts ready to leap out of their chests.

During the night Santo made love to her again—and again. He was a man who seriously needed to blot all other thoughts from his head, thought Penny. Not that she minded. This was a whole new experience. She had never been made love to so beautifully before, never been allowed to feel that her needs were important too.

After that first time he was a tender, considerate

lover and Penny couldn't believe that she was letting it happen. That the man she had thought was a hard, inconsiderate father was such a dream in bed.

Come morning, though, he had gone. The bed beside her was cold and empty. Immediately Penny felt guilt and shame. It spread across her like a rash. She had let him use her! She had let him see that she was his for the taking! Her stomach churned and anger and humiliation hit her full in the face.

She'd been incredibly stupid. How could she look him in the eye ever again? Perhaps she ought to leave before sleeping with her boss became the norm? Except that her duty lay with Chloe. She couldn't subject her to another series of nannies who revolted against the long hours Santo expected them to work.

By letting him take her to bed she had made a fool of herself but it wouldn't happen again, she would make sure of that. It would be strictly business from now on. She crept out of his room and towards her own, stopping to check on Chloe on the way. However, when she put her head around the door she saw that the little girl wasn't there.

Hopefully she'd be with her father. After what she'd told Santo he'd surely want to talk to his daughter, assure her that he loved her, that it was through no fault of his own that he'd never been around during those first years of her life.

Penny showered and dressed in double-quick time then, with her heart drumming, she went downstairs in search of them. She found Chloe in the kitchen with Emily, but no sign of Santo.

'Mr De Luca has gone to work,' informed the housekeeper.

'Did you see your daddy before he left?' Penny asked Chloe, and could hardly believe it when his daughter shook her head, her brown eyes revealing her disappointment.

Penny gave her a hug. 'He's such a busy man, I expect he didn't want to wake you. What are you having for breakfast?'

All day long Penny felt anger towards Santo. Not only for what he'd done to his daughter, but also because she'd made a fool of herself. He'd used her and she hated him for it. Except that he hadn't actually done that, had he? She'd been a more than willing partner. She'd wanted him as much as he'd wanted her, letting the sadness of the moment influence her.

When he didn't come home early enough to spend time with Chloe before she went to bed Penny was fuming, and it was almost ten before she heard his car on the driveway. She'd sat in silence, not watching TV, not playing music or even reading, she wanted to launch her attack the second he walked through the door. She knew his routine. He'd drop his briefcase in his study, hang his jacket on the back of a chair ready to take upstairs later and then move through into the smallest of the living rooms, where he'd pour himself a glass of whisky before relaxing in his favourite leather armchair.

He looked tired as he entered the room but Penny didn't care. She jumped up from her window seat and faced him. He smiled, unaware of the anger seething inside her. 'Penny. You looked so comfortable this morning that I didn't want to wake you. Hell, I've had a bad day.' He raked a hand through his hair, spiking it so that he looked younger than his thirty-six years, took off his tie, released his cuff-links and rolled back his shirtsleeves. 'How about you? What sort of a day have you had?' He walked over to her, looking prepared to take her into his arms. 'And Chloe? Is she in bed? I'd hoped to—'

'You'd hoped to what?' demanded Penny, unable to hold back a flood of anger.

'See her before she went to bed, of course.' He frowned and halted, sensing that all was not as he'd hoped it would be.

No doubt, thought Penny, he expected to carry on where he'd left off last night. If that was the case he was in for a big shock. 'That's very noble of you,' she shot fiercely, 'but she's been in bed hours. Do you have no idea what time it is? What was wrong with going in to work a little later this morning and talking to her before she went to school? Don't you care that your daughter thinks you don't love her?'

'Of course I care.' Confusion pulled his brows together. He clearly hadn't expected this attack.

'It doesn't look like it to me.' Penny's eyes flared fiercely into his face as she forget for a moment that she was his employee, that her livelihood depended on him. 'From where I'm standing you couldn't care less about Chloe. Find someone to look after her and she'll be all right; that's your maxim. You're not a father. You're simply a provider.'

His brow darkened. 'How dare you speak to me like that? You have no idea what I'm going through at this very moment.'

Penny lifted an expressive eyebrow. 'Perhaps I don't. But I know what Chloe's going through and she needs you more than your business does.'

Santo damned her with his dark eyes. All the passion and pleasure that she'd seen there last night was gone, leaving in its place a hard, cold man who didn't appreciate being told off by his daughter's nanny. After flaying her with another glance he strode across the room and poured himself a drink, taking a long swallow before facing her again.

'It's hard to believe you're the same woman who slept with me last night.'

Eyes that were black met her true blue ones, and Penny ignored the faint awareness that trickled through her veins. 'That's because I'm not the same woman,' she retorted. 'That woman was foolish. She gave in to emotional blackmail. She saw you were hurt and she wanted to help you through the pain. But this woman—' she clapped a hand to her heart '—sees the other side of you. The uncaring side. The workaholic. The man who puts his business before his family. I'm sure you'll agree it's not a pretty picture.'

CHAPTER FIVE

SANTO knew he ought to have spoken to Chloe before he went to work but he hadn't wanted to wake her at such an early hour. And because he'd been waiting for an international call, the time difference meant that he had made it home late. It didn't mean to say that he didn't feel deeply guilty; he did. He felt too awful for words. But what he didn't need now was a fire-breathing dragon telling him about it.

'You dare to criticise me?' Anger began to take the place of disbelief. No other employee had ever dared speak to him in this way. Not that he'd ever taken an employee to bed before! But this was a totally different person from the one who'd so fierily fed his hunger last night.

Penny's chin rose and her eyes flared. 'I definitely do dare. You don't deserve Chloe. Perhaps that's why your—' A swift hand went to her lips and she stopped abruptly.

But Santo knew what she'd been going to say. And she was right; his work ethics had been one of the reasons his wife had left him. But he sure as hell wasn't going to let anyone else criticise his behaviour.

Nevertheless he couldn't help but notice how beautiful she looked in her anger. Her blazing eyes were more purple than blue, her cheeks flushed, her breasts rising and falling as her breathing deepened. She wore some ridiculously thin, silky, soft blouse and a swift surge of raw need raced through him.

He'd been looking forward to coming home. Penny had been an exciting lover last night and he'd wanted more of her. He'd never met anyone with such an incredible appetite, who seemed to know instinctively how to pleasure him, how to take him to the brink time and time again before finally tipping him over the edge.

'I'll ignore that comment,' he told her tersely, 'and if you've quite finished telling me off about my daughter perhaps you'd care to join me in a drink—perhaps we can talk this through rationally?' His male hormones were fuelled by the fire in her incredibly eloquent eyes. They damned him, but heaven help him, he wanted her in his bed again tonight.

One taste of Penelope Keeling and he'd become an addict. Normally when he was at work he never thought about anything except the job in hand. He kept the two parts of his life strictly separate. But today, even though the meeting was of paramount importance, he'd found his mind wandering.

Visions of long, wavy blonde hair spreading out over his chest and loins caused his breath to catch in his throat. Erotic images of her tempting little kisses getting ever closer to his manhood made him feel hard. He'd even thought he could still smell the heady scent of her on his skin.

Although he'd managed with a Herculean effort to banish such wanton thoughts, the feelings had returned with a vengeance as he'd made his way home.

Penny couldn't believe Santo's audacity. She stood and faced him, her breathing all over the place, wondering how she could have ever given herself to him. The man had no heart; he was driven by work. Pleasure was something to be squeezed in between. And as for his daughter—well, words failed her.

She would have thought that after losing out for so many years he'd want to spend every hour of every day with her. She couldn't weigh him up at all.

'You really think I'd have a drink with you after—after everything?' Penny curled her fingers into fists, ignoring the pounding of her heart and the heat filming her skin. 'You're unbelievable. I'm going to bed. Goodnight, Mr De Luca.' She spun on her heel and walked away.

'I think not.'

His words were a command. Automatically Penny stopped. And very slowly she turned around. 'You have no right to dictate what I do in my own time. I'm not employed to socialise with you. Or did I get the picture wrong?' she questioned, her voice full of sarcasm. 'Is that what you had in mind all along?'

'The hell I didn't and you know it,' he threw back at her.

'Chloe was your main concern?'

'Exactly.'

'Then you have your answer,' she returned fiercely. 'Chloe is my principal concern as well. Last night was a one-off; it will not happen again.'

And this time when she walked away he did not try to stop her.

Penny threw herself down on the bed and wondered at her temerity in speaking to Santo the way she had. It was a wonder he hadn't dismissed her on the spot.

But she wasn't sorry for what she'd said; she meant every word.

Through the window she could see an almost full moon, and as she hadn't bothered to switch on the light it bathed everything in cool silver, enhancing the elegance of the room. Penny knew she ought to feel lucky that she'd landed herself a job in a place like this.

It had been wrong of her to give in to temptation. One half of her still fancied Santo like mad and wanted to repeat the experience, the other half couldn't accept the way he behaved towards Chloe. She felt a fierce protective urge towards the child every time she thought about it, like a mother hen looking after its brood.

In the middle of the night Penny woke up and realised that she was still fully dressed. Quietly she slid off the bed and crossed to the bathroom—pausing when she heard the sound of voices.

It sounded like Chloe and Santo—in Chloe's room!

She tiptoed to the adjoining door and listened. Yes, it was definitely father and daughter. A faint smile curved her lips. She was tempted to go in and say something, but she didn't. She undressed and slipped back into bed instead.

All was quiet when she got up the next morning. She found Chloe downstairs in the breakfast room—with her father! The man who always left for work at seven…and it was now a quarter to eight! Penny walked in and smiled. 'Good morning.'

Chloe giggled.

'Do come and join us,' invited Santo.

Penny raised her brows at him. 'Thank you.' And took her seat.

There was not a lot she could say in front of his

daughter, but she let her approval show. And when he eventually said that he had to leave for work she nodded coolly. Chloe on the other hand gave him a big hug, and he kissed her on both cheeks, which was the first time Penny had seen him show such emotion.

'Did you know that Chloe breaks up for the summer holidays on Friday?' Penny had been enjoying the pleasures of the garden when Santo arrived home. It was one of those hot, sultry evenings when everything was still, when the perfume of the flowers hung heavy in the air, when even the birds were silent.

She'd found a bench by the lake—where already a fence had been erected—and was watching some squabbling ducks when Santo surprised her by joining her. His business suit was gone, replaced by a sky-blue shirt and a pair of casual trousers. His dark hair, still wet from a shower, looked as though all he'd done was run his fingers through it. Gone was the suave businessman, in its place was a relaxed, gorgeously handsome Italian who smelled exotic and sexy and set every one of her nerve-ends on fire.

'She does? Why didn't I know of this earlier?'

'I imagine you had a calendar at the beginning of the year,' she said, lifting her brows, wishing he hadn't sat quite so close. How could she possibly ignore him? How could she stem the flood of feelings that had begun to race through her body?

Santo's frown was almost comical. 'It was never passed on to me.'

And would you have remembered if it had been? wondered Penny. Santo was too tied up in his own world. He'd probably disposed of it in his waste bin.

'It means she'll be at home for six weeks,' said Penny.

'And—the reason you're telling me is?' he questioned. 'Surely you're not thinking of taking time off yourself?' A faint frown accompanied his words and Penny was fascinated by the two tiny furrows in his brow. She felt an urge to smooth them away with the tips of her fingers. She almost ached to touch him—which was crazy under the circumstances.

'Of course not,' she answered. 'But if you don't mind me saying so I would suggest that you take some time off yourself. Take Chloe away. A beach holiday somewhere; just the two of you. You need to bond with her and it would be an ideal opportunity.'

Penny held her breath as she waited for his answer. She expected an explosion. A 'who, me?' scenario. And she deliberately averted her eyes, went back to watching the ducks.

Not that she wasn't conscious of him; too much so. The very air around her had changed. It had thickened until breathing was virtually impossible. Santo's presence was everywhere. She would never have believed that one man could fill such a large space.

And when the silence between them lengthened, when she could wait for his answer no longer, Penny turned to him—and felt a shock wave rip through her. He was looking at her with such an intense expression in his velvety brown eyes that she couldn't breathe, couldn't even move.

'An excellent idea, Penny.'

Goodness. Had he really said that?

'You're right, we do need time together.'

So far so good!

'But there is one problem.'

Here we go! The excuse! The get-out!

'Chloe needs you as well.'

'What?' The word was out before she could stop it. Chloe needed her! More likely *he* needed her. An excuse to get her back into his bed.

'There are things you do for her that I'm no good at.'

'Then you'll have to learn,' she declared firmly, trying not to look into those magnetic eyes. Finding it impossible. He was so close, so vital, that she was trapped like a fly in a spider's web. 'If I come along it will defeat the whole objective.' And she glared at him, trying to feel nothing except contempt for his suggestion.

'And if you don't come along and I fail her, what then?'

'Are you blackmailing me, Mr De Luca?' Penny deliberately addressed him formally, seeing this as the only way she could keep their conversation on an even keel. Because, lord help her, she wanted him. And she was desperately afraid that it might show.

'Would I dare?' His lips twitched as he spoke.

He was different tonight, thought Penny. She was seeing a softer side to his character—or was it because he was after something? Because he wanted her back in his bed. Whatever, it was having an alarming effect on her senses. She ought to move, walk a few steps away; pull herself together.

But she didn't. She couldn't. She was immobilised. 'You're capable of anything,' she told him, and hoped he didn't hear the alarming tremble in her voice.

'That's something on which we both agree,' he told her, 'and at this very moment I do believe I'm capable of kissing my daughter's very attractive nanny.'

Even though he had warned her, even though she knew his intent, Penny still didn't move. She watched his face draw closer, saw the dangerous darkness in his eyes, inhaled the intoxicating male smell of him, felt excitement hurtle through her veins.

Ever nearer he came, stopping only when his mouth was millimetres away from hers. Penny held her breath and waited, locking her eyes into his. She knew what he was doing. He was tormenting her. Waiting to see whether she'd take the initiative or whether she'd back away.

Her palms grew sweaty and her heart pounded, and she wanted his kisses more than anything else, but common sense prevailed. From somewhere deep inside her came the strength to resist. She leaned backwards from the hips, blue eyes flashing. 'I think not,' she told him bravely, 'and if you think this is a good way of persuading me to join you on holiday then you're very much mistaken.'

To her annoyance he smiled and, with a faint you-win-some-you-lose-some shrug, he relaxed back against the bench.

Santo didn't know from where he'd found the strength to put distance between him and Penny. When he had arrived home and found Chloe asleep but no Penny he'd been disappointed, until Emily had told him that she was outside. And he'd come out here with one purpose in mind: to kiss her.

She had surprised him with the information that Chloe's school was closing for their annual holidays. He supposed that at some time he'd been told but he had completely forgotten about it. And his first thought had been thank goodness for Penny.

But when she'd mentioned taking Chloe away—just

the two of them—he'd not been happy. Yes, it would be a good way of bonding with his daughter, as Penny so eloquently put it, but coping with an active five-year-old on his own wouldn't be easy. He'd need help. And if Penny came too it would make all the difference. Penny in his bed every night would more than compensate.

Not that he expected she would fall easily into his arms. She'd been scared by the depth of her emotions during the night they'd spent together. Initially she'd wanted to comfort him—but who had enjoyed themselves the most in what followed afterwards was a moot question.

'It seems like I'll have to find some other form of persuasion,' he told her softly, stroking back a stray strand of hair where it clung to her cheek, allowing his fingers to linger, to feel the downy softness of her skin. He couldn't remember the last time a woman had got through to him like this.

Penny was different in every way to any other woman he'd known. It was a change for him to be rejected. Not that he wanted to take her for that reason alone. He wasn't that bloody-minded. But she was intriguing as well as a fantastic lover. She blew hot and cold and didn't mind telling him off. Something he'd never experienced before.

He'd had arguments with his wife but they had been different. They had been mainly about money—and how fast she spent it. Money didn't seem to be a factor where Penny was concerned. Yes, she'd needed the job, she'd been overwhelmed when he said how much he was prepared to pay her, but she hadn't tried to wheedle her way into his bed.

If anything it was the other way round. And he

wasn't succeeding. Which was proving to be something of a challenge. Especially when she knocked his hand away from her face, saying crossly, 'Santo De Luca, you're going the right way to make me walk out of this job.'

He frowned then and drew back his hand. 'You don't like me touching you any more?'

Penny closed her eyes and he saw the tussle she was having with herself. 'What I like and what is proper are two different things,' she said crossly. 'For one thing, I'm in your employ and the way I see it there should be no crossing over of loyalties. And also, I'm not interested in an affair—with any man.'

'Care to tell me who made you feel this way?' She sounded so passionate, so vehement that he was intrigued. And he wanted to know who had done this to her.

But Penny shook her head. 'It's no one's business but mine. It's not something I want to talk about, ever.'

'He hurt you that much?'

She lifted her slender shoulders. 'I guess.'

Santo felt a surge of anger that any man could take advantage of such a warm, caring person. Warm and caring? Where had that come from? Fire and brimstone was a better description. Or was it the other side of her that he was seeing? She was an intriguing combination and he wanted to get to know her a whole lot better.

But more than that he wanted to pull her into his arms and comfort her, except that he knew she'd take it the wrong way. So he pushed himself to his feet and walked to the water's edge, turning to look back at her. 'Care to change your mind on the holiday idea?'

He made himself sound hopeful and wistful, slanting her a wry smile. 'If I take Chloe I really could do with your help—purely as her nanny, of course.' As for anything else, well, he'd see what happened. He was not looking for a permanent relationship—like Penny, once bitten, twice shy—but he didn't see why they couldn't indulge in an affair.

Penny found herself wavering. Of course she wanted to go. And more than anything she wanted to share Santo's bed again. But where would it lead? She didn't want to get hurt again.

On the other hand she wasn't sure that Santo was up to looking after his daughter full-time. Not on his own.

Or was she being unfair? Doing him an injustice?

She looked at him for several long moments. He had a little-boy-lost expression, his gorgeous mouth turned down slightly at the corners, his eyes sad, and although Penny knew it was solely for her benefit she couldn't help but be won over.

What she wanted to do was smile widely, run over to him and fling herself into his arms, declaring that yes, she would join him. But that would be tantamount to declaring a willingness to indulge in an affair. And she knew in her heart of hearts that she wasn't capable of taking the pleasure and then walking away. It needed to be all or nothing.

And Santo was offering her nothing.

'I'm still waiting,' he said softly. 'If you can't do it for my sake then think of Chloe.'

Penny gave a wistful smile. He knew he'd get her on the Chloe issue. She gave the faintest of nods. 'For Chloe's sake.'

Immediately he grinned.

She'd not seen so much pleasure on his face before. Pleasure when they were making love, yes—but that had been entirely different. This was childish pleasure. It made her beam too.

'I think a celebration's in order,' he announced. 'Come.' And before she could object he took her hand and led her back to the house.

Penny wanted to snatch her hand away but felt it would be churlish, and when he almost ran across the lawns she started to laugh. Santo laughed too and when they burst into the house she half expected him to swing her around in his arms and kiss her.

But he didn't and she was glad because it would have ruined everything. This was a side to Santo she hadn't seen before, and she liked it. He was fun. And in the beginning fun wasn't a word she would ever have used to describe him.

He left her in the garden room, pushing the doors open wide to let in the pleasant evening air, returning a few minutes later with a bottle of champagne and two elegant crystal flutes.

Watching as he filled their glasses, Penny couldn't help admiring his long, slender fingers—fingers that had touched and excited every inch of her body, that excited her again now just thinking about the pleasure he'd given her! And she knew that she'd need to be careful and not drink too much or she'd end up in his bed again tonight.

And that would set a precedent for the holiday.

'Have you had any thoughts where you'd like to take Chloe?' Mentioning his daughter's name felt a safe thing to do. 'Somewhere in Cornwall would be nice. In Looe children sit on the harbour wall dangling crab lines into the water. She'd love that. And there are good beaches in the area as well.'

Santo handed Penny her drink and raised his glass to hers, waiting until she'd taken her first sip before answering. 'I'm going to take you somewhere—you and Chloe,' he amended quickly, 'where I used to go as a boy.'

'In Italy?' asked Penny quickly, not missing his slip of the tongue but choosing to ignore it.

He nodded. 'Have you ever been there?'

'No,' she admitted with a tiny rueful smile, 'though it's a place I've always wanted to visit, especially Rome.'

'Yes, Rome.'

He said the name with an odd inflection in his voice, and his beautiful accent deepened. It made him even sexier and Penny felt her throat tighten. 'Do you miss Italy?'

'Sometimes, but I love England too. My mother was English.'

'Was?' questioned Penny softly.

'Sadly she's no longer alive.' His eyes clouded over briefly. 'She was born and lived right here in London. She met my father here. But he wouldn't leave his beloved Italy. I had no such compunction. I studied at Oxford and have stayed ever since.'

'And your father—is he—?'

'He lives in Rome still and will until the day he dies.' A shuttered look crossed Santo's face before he continued. 'But enough about me and my family,' he said firmly. 'Let's concentrate on us.'

Us? Penny shivered inwardly, aware that she'd need to be on her guard while they were away. Nor could she help wondering why she'd given in to temptation in the first place.

Because, came the answer, Santo De Luca is one hell of a sexy man. How could anyone resist him?

But resist him she'd need to. She took another sip of her champagne, and then another, and before she knew it she'd finished the whole glass and Santo was refilling it.

'Please, no more,' she said faintly, but the alcohol was already beginning to take effect.

'We can't waste the bottle,' he declared. 'And the night's young. There's no rush.'

Penny sucked in a breath. What was he expecting?

CHAPTER SIX

A WHOLE week had passed since Santo asked Penny to join him and Chloe in Italy. Her emotions had see-sawed; she'd gone from an absolute declaration that she wouldn't go to an out-and-out anticipation of the event that flooded her body with secret delight.

It was Chloe's enthusiasm that had clinched it for her. The little girl had been so excited after her father told her where they were going that she'd been physically sick and there were fears that they wouldn't make it.

Now they were flying over the Swiss Alps in Santo's private jet and Chloe was watching through the window. Each time she turned to look at them her eyes were as wide as saucers. There was no hiding her happiness.

'No regrets?' asked Santo quietly, one eye on his daughter but the other fixed firmly on Penny.

'None at all,' answered Penny.

Actually she was looking forward to the holiday almost as much as Chloe. She so wanted to see everything that she'd read about in history books or seen on television. This was going to be the real thing—and with a gorgeous Italian to show her around. What more could she ask for?

During the past week Santo had kept a respectable distance. He still maintained his long hours, though there had been a couple of occasions when he had surprised her by coming home early. He also tried to make sure that he saw his daughter before he went out to work each morning. He was making an effort and for that she thanked him.

When he did come home early they spent time together, usually outside, sharing a bottle of wine, and she knew that he was wondering whether he dared kiss her again. She tried to give him no encouragement, except that it was hard with her emotions running high!

She had only to catch sight of him to feel a rush of desire, a trembling in her limbs and an unbearable heat in her lower abdomen. It was sometimes more than she could bear and it was all she could do to hide her feelings. At least she hoped that she did. There had been a time when she'd caught Santo looking at her strangely and realised that she was in grave danger.

'I'm eternally grateful that the agency sent you to me,' he'd said softly, his voice little more than a throb.

'You mean I'm better at my job than the others?' she had asked, deliberately misunderstanding.

'That too,' he'd agreed.

But it was the words he didn't say that had made Penny's heart spin.

Nevertheless they'd made it through the week without him attempting to kiss her, or even touch her again. Not that he hadn't made love to her. His eyes had seduced and her body had erupted traitorously. Not once but several times. It was something she would never have thought possible, not in a million years.

The plane had surprised her, though it shouldn't

have. She'd never actually thought about it; if she had she would have guessed that the likes of Santo De Luca had their own private jet.

The cabin was as sumptuous as a king's palace with deep leather armchairs and a marble-topped table. One would be spoilt for choice from a well-stocked bookcase, and in a corner was a computer console so that business could be conducted throughout the whole flight. There was even a bedroom.

Penny's mind had balked when Santo had shown her; she'd taken one swift look and backed out again.

An eyebrow had risen and she knew exactly what he had been thinking. Had they been alone it went without saying that the whole flight would have been spent exploring its possibilities. Thank goodness for Chloe!

This was Chloe's holiday, not hers, not to be spent enjoying herself with Santo, but ensuring that his daughter had a good time.

And he needed to do that too. She had frequently told him so and it looked as though he was finally taking her at her word. He'd ensured that Chloe had a good stock of toys to keep her occupied when she tired of travelling, and he'd talked to her a lot about what they planned to do.

'Do you know,' he said, interrupting Penny's thoughts, 'I haven't had a holiday for as long as I can remember? How about you? When was the last time you went away?'

Penny smiled. 'Last year actually. I went to Corsica with a group of friends.' And when he raised a questioning brow, she added, 'It was a hen party.' And thought she saw relief on his face.

In reality it shouldn't have bothered him who she holidayed with. Except that she sensed Santo had a pro-

prietorial air about him these days. And it scared her.
Making love with him had been a big mistake. She
could never look into his face again without remember-
ing those magical, heart-stopping moments. The link
had been created; it would be impossible to break. Only
time and distance could do that—and she was reluctant
to leave her job, even though she knew it could well
come to that.

'I'm looking forward to Rome,' she said, needing to
rescue the situation.

'Rome?' His eyes widened. 'I didn't say we were
going there. We're going to a place in the Bay of Naples.
Chloe will love it.'

'But—don't you want to go and see your father? I
thought he lived in Rome,' she asked gently, knowing
that this was a subject Santo didn't like talking about.

'No, I do not.' A deep scowl darkened his brow,
making him look stern and forbidding. 'In fact I'd rather
we didn't talk about him. Please don't mention him
again.'

Penny knew she had hit a raw nerve and thought
back to other times she had tried to broach the subject
of Santo's family. She realised that she knew hardly
anything about the man seated next to her and the
subject of his father clearly upset him. Penny couldn't
imagine what it would be like not to want to spend time
with your father. Surely his father would need him more
than ever, since his mother had died? But if Santo didn't
want to go and see him, or even talk about him, then
who was she to argue?

Penny had loved both her parents dearly, and could
never imagine falling out with either one of them. And
now that they were gone she was glad that they'd never

had cross words. It must be uncomfortable to know that you were a sworn enemy of the person who had pro-created you. How could it be? How could anything be so bad that you didn't even want to talk about him?

'Look, aeroplanes,' cried Chloe, pointing out of the window.

Penny gave a faint sigh of relief when she looked down and saw that they were almost at their destination.

The heat met them as they alighted from the aircraft, but in no time they were whisked away in a chauffeur-driven, air-conditioned car.

Chloe insisted on sitting between them, which was something of a relief as far as Penny was concerned because the long hours sitting in Santo's company had sizzled her senses. She was more aware of him than she'd ever been—and even began to wonder whether it had been wise to suggest this holiday.

Except that she'd done it in all good faith. Not for one moment had she anticipated Santo suggesting she accompany them. But he had, and she was here, and a whole week lay ahead of them—maybe longer—and she didn't know what he expected of her.

There was little chance of conversation, Chloe did all the chattering, pointing out everything that was fasci-nating and different, until finally they pulled up in front of a pair of electronically operated gates that opened on their arrival. Once out of the car they were whisked upwards in a lift set into the hillside to an amazing open terrace. And right in front of them was the villa.

Penny could only stand and stare. 'This is where you holidayed as a child?' Not only was it huge, with windows and balconies overlooking the turquoise waters below, but its architecture was stunning also.

White walls that dazzled, arches, pillars, even some castellation. It was truly magnificent. 'Does it belong to your family?' she asked in awe.

Even Chloe was lost for words.

'It's my grandfather's—or was; he died last year. My father owns it now but he doesn't come here himself. He keeps it for any one of his relatives or friends who wishes to use it.'

So he had at least been in touch with his father, thought Penny, though wisely she said nothing. 'It's out of this world.'

Santo smiled. 'I'd actually forgotten how splendid it is. When I was a child I have to confess it seemed much bigger. I expect Chloe thinks it's enormous, don't you, *mio bello*?'

Chloe smiled from ear to ear and nodded. 'Is it a fairy castle?'

'It's everything and anything that you want it to be,' he agreed. 'Shall we explore?'

Chloe nodded energetically and took Santo's offered hand.

Penny felt a glow of satisfaction. It looked as though this holiday was going to be the turning point in Santo's relationship with his daughter—exactly what she had hoped for.

The villa had more rooms than they would ever use, more bathrooms, more of everything in fact; three terraces, two with swimming pools, both fenced, she was pleased to see. They even had their own private beach.

There was also a maid and a cook, and a handyman who looked after the gardens and the pools. It was sheer luxury and nothing like Penny had expected.

Tired after their long journey, Chloe had climbed on her bed and immediately fallen asleep.

'I suggest a drink,' announced Santo as they left her room. 'We'll take it on the terrace and discuss the view.'

'I need to unpack.' Penny felt her heart give a sudden jerk. She knew what view he meant.

'The maid will do it,' he assured her, 'that's what she's here for. What is wrong? You do not want my company?'

There was a faint sound of irritation in his voice and Penny shook her head. 'I can't help but remember that I'm your employee. It's not proper that I should spend so much time with you.'

'So what would you propose you do?' he enquired, an eyebrow raised, eyes closely watching her reaction.

Penny shrugged.

'There, you see. You have nothing to do but keep me company. It is both my wish and my pleasure. Come.' He took her elbow and led her outside, where they sat in wicker armchairs beneath a huge canopy. The ocean was a mixture of delicate blues and greens, dotted by the occasional white sail, and on the horizon she could just make out the shape of a liner.

All was tranquil except for the fast beat of her heart. Bougainvillea trailed over a low wall and hibiscus grew in tubs. It was the fairy-tale palace Chloe had claimed. Never in a million years had Penny ever dreamt that she would one day holiday in a place like this.

'It's very beautiful,' she said with a faint smile.

'I thought you would like it.'

'And you haven't been here since you were a boy?'

'No.' He allowed himself a faintly nostalgic smile. 'Life got in the way. University, building my business.

I had no time for holidays. And I wouldn't be here now if it wasn't for your insistence.'

Her smile widened. 'Then I'm glad I pushed you.' And her heart did amazing somersaults when he flashed his white teeth in an answering smile. Even his eyes softened, looking at her with something near to tenderness.

'Your drinks, Signor.' The maid appeared silently at their sides.

Penny was glad of the interruption and watched the girl as she slid a jug and two glasses onto the low table in front of them, together with a dish of olives, and then disappeared as quietly as she had come.

Santo leaned forward and filled her glass with the delicious-looking fruit juice and Penny was glad it wasn't anything stronger. It would be so easy to drink too much here in this place of blazing blue skies and fantastic surroundings—to say nothing of the company!

But when she tasted the juice Penny found that it wasn't what she'd expected. There was a definite taste of alcohol. She looked at Santo with a frown chasing across her normally smooth forehead.

'You don't like?'

'What is it?'

'Fruit punch, I think you would call it. Made to an old family recipe. It is very refreshing.'

'And intoxicating,' she accused.

'Too much and it will go to your head, I agree,' he said. 'But is that a bad thing? We have had a long day; we deserve to relax and enjoy.'

Penny picked up an olive and bit it in half, looking at the piece that remained between her fingers as though it was of paramount interest. Anything so she didn't have to look at Santo. 'You make it sound as though you and I are here on holiday together, not as employer and employee.'

'Is that how you want it to be?' asked Santo, a sudden edge to his voice. 'You do not want to be friends?'

Penny dared to look at him and saw the frown slashing his brow. She felt a rush of unease. Of course she wanted more. That one taste had caused a hunger that only he could assuage. But brief affairs, because that was all it would be, were not for her. She couldn't give her body to any man who wasn't seriously interested in a long-term relationship—ideally marriage. And she knew that Santo had no intention of ever getting married again.

She ignored the tiny voice in her head that said she had already given herself to him. That had been a one-off, never to be repeated. If anything had been dangerous it was that. A foolish error of judgement. She had only wanted to comfort him.

'We can hardly help being anything other than friends, can we,' she said, 'when we both have Chloe's best interests at heart?'

'I love my daughter,' he acknowledged, his gorgeous brown eyes terrifyingly watchful on hers, 'and I know you're very fond of her already. But we both have a life outside Chloe.'

'Naturally,' agreed Penny, 'I'm here as Chloe's nanny. You're her father. That's it, that's what we are.'

'So if I said that I want you in my bed again you'd refuse?'

It was the way his voice had seductively lowered that sent the shivers through her body. The way his eyes made love to her. And she knew that she was doomed. It was going to be impossible to resist this totally gorgeous Italian.

And when he spoke again in his own language, when the words sounded so romantic and exciting, Penny knew that she was lost. Nevertheless she spoke firmly. 'It was a mistake I'm not likely to repeat.'

But there was no conviction behind her words and Santo knew it. She could see the speculation in his eyes, the knowledge that he was going to enjoy the chase as much as the capitulation.

Santo was well aware of the fact that he'd insisted Penny accompany him and Chloe because he wanted— no, correction, because he *needed* her company. He thought about her constantly, his body demanded fulfilment, and having her at his side but knowing that he could not reach out and touch, and take, was driving him crazy.

It was early days but he hoped that the ambience here, coupled with the beautiful weather and the fact that he'd be her constant companion, would bring to him again the fantastically uninhibited woman who had shared his bed. If they'd gone to his father's place then he might as well have left her at home. There was nothing there that was conducive to romance.

His lips thinned for a moment as memories he'd tried to bury rose once again to the surface. Determinedly he dashed them away. He wanted nothing to destroy their pleasure. One day he might let them take hold. But not now. 'Drink,' he ordered, gesturing towards her glass, and he was pleased when she took a sip, and then another.

'You like?'

'It's lovely,' she agreed, 'but I'm not going to forget that it's alcoholic.'

'Just a little,' he declared with a careless wave of his hand. 'Nothing to worry about. You won't get drunk.

Tell me more about yourself, about your childhood. You say your father died when you were—how old?'

'Five,' she said.

'Chloe's age. That is sad,' he acknowledged.

'And it's also why I'm urging you to spend more time with your own daughter,' said Penny urgently. 'They are such important years. You want her to remember every one of them with pleasure. My father and I did some wonderful things together. He always seemed to be playing with me, taking me out, buying me little treats—not that we had much money. But I'll never forget them.'

She spoke with such sincerity, such earnestness that Santo could picture in his mind Penny as a little girl with her father. He could see love and joy, friendship and fun, and the hurt deep down inside that Helena had denied him Chloe for the first years of her life grew excruciating.

Penny had opened his eyes to the fact that his daughter, his very own flesh and blood, was crying inside because he didn't know how to love her.

All of a sudden he wanted to rush inside and fold Chloe in his arms and tell her how much she meant to him. When she woke, yes, he would... Now, though, he had the beautiful Penny to keep him company. Beautiful and exciting.

Simply looking at her sent his male hormones into overdrive. He wanted to make love to her *now*! His whole body was sensitised, as though it was ready to explode at any minute. He'd never had to work so hard keeping himself in check.

'It sounds as though your father was a wonderful man.'

'He was,' she admitted easily. 'My mother went to pieces when he died. It was a car accident. He was there

one day, gone the next. She never had time to say
goodbye, to tell him how much she loved him. She in-
stilled in me and my sister the importance of telling a
person you love them. We said it to each other every day
after that until—' Penny's eyes filled with tears '—she
too died. She was ill a long time, so it wasn't unexpected, but even so it was hard. I still miss her.'

Santo couldn't help himself. In a heartbeat he closed
the space between them and, kneeling in front of her,
he took her into his arms.

Strong arms, thought Penny. He was comforting her
the way she had comforted him—and look where that
had led! But she didn't push him away. She allowed
herself the pleasure. She drank in the clean masculine
smell of him, letting it wash away her sadness, bring
back to reality the fact that he was the most exciting man
she had ever met.

When he let her go and returned to his seat she was
surprised. She had expected it to lead to a kiss, perhaps
something more, and contrarily was disappointed. But
what he didn't do with words and actions he did with
his eyes. Velvety brown eyes made love to her. They undressed her and made love to her. She could feel it in
every part of her body.

Half-hidden by lowered eyelids, they searched and
found each intimate area. Her nipples hardened and
stung so much that she wanted to protect them with her
hands, every one of her sensitive spots was on high
alert, and when her groin grew unbearably responsive,
when she couldn't help wriggling in her seat, she knew
she had to create a diversion.

A drink, a long drink, she thought, and to hell with
the fact that it was laced with alcohol. To her horror her

hand shook so much that she knocked the glass over. Mortified—she hadn't wanted to create that kind of distraction—she lifted the glass, only to have Santo's hand close over hers.

'Leave it,' he said, his voice low and gruff. 'Isabella will clean it up.'

As if the maid had been hovering she appeared on silent feet, taking the glass away and bringing another, mopping up the spilt drink. Penny was embarrassed, Santo on the other hand acted as though nothing untoward had happened.

Did he know, she wondered, that her clumsiness was a result of his mental lovemaking? That her body was achingly aware of him and if she didn't get away soon she would end up in his bed? Heaven help her if this torment was going to last the whole holiday.

'I'd like to explore,' she said, dismayed to hear how husky her voice sounded. She felt as if she was enclosed in a prison of her own making. There was no air to breathe, no space to move. Only Santo! All around her. Consuming her, feeding her, sensitising her. Doing everything in his power to entice her into his bed.

She was weak, treacherously so, and she wanted time to herself but it wasn't to be. 'Good idea,' declared Santo, jumping to his feet. 'Come, I will show you the delights this place has to offer.'

He held out his hand but she ignored it, trailing alongside him instead. At the other end of the terrace was a dining area with a table for up to eight people. Would they entertain? wondered Penny. Or would it be just the three of them the whole time?

Through a gate and down some steps was another terrace where a large kidney-shaped pool sparkled invitingly in the sunlight. At its side was an impressive array of sun beds. But more tempting still was a hydro massage tub. Penny could just imagine sitting in it enjoying the view while her body was stimulated and relaxed at the same time.

Santo saw her eyeing it. 'Shall we?' he asked softly.

Together! The two of them! Penny shook her head. Too intimate, too everything. She needed distance from Santo, not intimacy.

But intimacy was what she got when he pressed a button in the wall, a door she had not noticed slid open and he stepped back for her to enter.

'What's this?' she asked suspiciously.

'A lift down to the beach. I thought you might enjoy a walk along the shore, we might find a sea breeze there. It can be stifling on the terraces.'

Penny nodded. 'It is hot.' The doors closed silently and they were entombed in their own private space. She forgot to breathe. She held herself rigid against one of the cool metal walls and closed her eyes.

'You don't like lifts?' Santo's concerned voice entered her consciousness.

'No, I was stuck in one once for three hours.' It didn't bother her any more and she hadn't even thought about it before he asked. But at least it was an excuse.

Immediately his arms came around her and she was held firmly against him. 'You should have said, there are steps. A lot of steps, admittedly—it's a long way down—but…'

Penny wasn't listening, at least not to his voice, but to the strong beat of his heart against her. To her own throbbing in unison. She prayed they'd arrive quickly. It suited her to let him think that she was panicking because of the lift; she didn't want him to know that he was the one who'd dealt her senses such death-defying blows.

But when his mouth claimed hers Penny knew that she was lost.

CHAPTER SEVEN

ON A SCALE of one to ten Santo's kiss rated about thirteen. Penny forgot where she was, aware of nothing except the taste of his lips, the feel of his hard, exciting body against hers, the way the blood raced through her veins as though someone was in hot pursuit. She actually found herself urging her hips closer, returning his kiss with an abandonment that she knew she would regret later.

Was it the confined space that made her act like this? The knowledge that no one could see them? Up until now she'd been determined not to repeat the kiss that had shown her exactly how deeply Santo could affect her senses.

He was an undisputed expert in the kissing stakes. He made her feel special. He was sending her mindless with desire. The scent of him was all-enveloping in this tiny vacuum, it flooded her senses, invaded and controlled.

Her arms laced around his neck, fingers threading through the thickness of his hair, pulling his head even closer, her lips parting beneath the onslaught. Their tongues danced around each other, touching, tasting, teasing, until Penny's body screamed out for more.

Even when the lift stopped, when she sensed that they were no longer falling in space, she didn't struggle for freedom. It was crazed insanity but there was something inside her that refused to let go.

'You're safe now.' Santo's voice broke the spell—plus the fact that the lift doors opened and a blast of hot air swept in.

Feeling dazed after the intensity of her emotions Penny backed out of his embrace and took a faltering step forward. Immediately his arm steadied her. 'I'm sorry,' said Penny.

'For what?' One corner of Santo's mouth curved upwards in amusement. 'For kissing me or for feeling afraid in a lift? The way I see it, if the kiss took your mind off your fear then it did its job and you have nothing to apologise for.'

'I shouldn't have let you.' It had been a bad mistake. One that could have disastrous consequences. It had told him how easily she could be manipulated. And she was afraid that this one kiss might lead to something more.

Santo was irresistible, there were no two ways about it. And here in this magical place it was going to be incredibly hard pretending indifference. Would she even want to? He was the sexiest man she had ever met; he did things to her that should never be allowed.

Crazily she hadn't wanted the kiss to stop, she had wanted more. She had wanted to feel his hot kisses on other parts of her body; she had wanted to touch him, to feel his need, to feed the hunger growing inside her, to bring it to its ultimate, mind-blowing conclusion.

She felt bereft now, as though she'd been given the taste of a golden prize and then had it snatched away. She felt strangely uncoordinated, her legs not carrying her as steadily as they should. Her mind searched for something to say, something to take her mind off this torment.

'Chloe,' she said urgently. 'What if she wakes? She's in a strange place; she'll—'

Promptly Santo stroked a gentle finger over her lips, stemming her flow of words, but in so doing creating a fresh flow of desire. 'You need not worry; Isabella will keep an eye on her.'

Penny sighed gently. She liked the feel of him, the taste of him, and she wanted to touch her tongue to his finger, she wanted to suck it into her mouth, to keep alive those feelings that had not yet gone away. But she didn't. Common sense prevailed. She moved away from him instead and began walking across the white sand. The beach was tiny and crescent-shaped and one half of her revelled in her fortune to be in such a wildly beautiful place, while the other half was deeply disturbed at the way her feelings were running out of control.

The azure ocean lapped gently at her feet and she kicked off her sandals and let the sand and water drift through her toes. She had an urge to throw off her clothes and swim naked in the warm waters. Of course she didn't, but she promised herself that one day she would sneak down and do just that.

The beach was private, backed by sheer cliffs clothed in green shrubs and trees that she felt sure must have a very tenuous hold. She couldn't even see the villa from here. It was like being alone in the world; a magical place.

'What are you thinking?'

Santo's gruff voice was close and she whirled around to find that only inches separated them. He too had taken off his shoes and socks and rolled up the legs of his light cotton trousers. He looked carefree; he had a very different persona from the dedicated businessman who found it difficult to spare time for his own daughter.

'How beautiful this part of the world is. You're very lucky.' And she ignored the racing of her heart, tried to pretend that his nearness hadn't once again affected her breathing.

'I'm lucky to have found you—for Chloe's sake,' he added. But his sensational dark eyes told her differently. They swept over her with amazing thoroughness, not missing an inch. Causing her to suck in her breath and attempt to ignore the hardening of her breasts and the crunch deep down in her belly.

It was hard though. How could you ignore a man as damningly sexy as Santo De Luca? Especially here in his home country, where he had become even more Italian. His accent had deepened and he seemed so at home with his surroundings that Penny couldn't understand why he had ever chosen to live in London.

'If this were mine,' she said with a wide sweep of her hand, 'I'd want to spend as much time here as possible.'

'Time is money as far as I'm concerned,' was his response.

'But everyone needs a holiday at least once a year.'

'Maybe if I'd had you for company,' he said softly, 'I'd have been persuaded before now.'

A fiery heat returned to fill her body with burning passion. 'Mr De Luca,' Penny drew herself up to her full height, still failing by several inches to match up, nevertheless doing the best she could to look imposing, 'I am your daughter's nanny, nothing more, and I'd appreciate it if you'd remember that.'

His gorgeously shaped lips twitched as he fought to hide a smile and Penny couldn't fail to acknowledge

that a few minutes ago, seconds even, they had been
staking a claim on hers. So beautifully. So intimately
and heart-stoppingly. Therefore how could she expect
him to take her comment seriously? And how could she
pretend that it was otherwise?

She had placed herself in a damning situation and she
couldn't see her way out of it.

'I think,' he said, stroking a strand of hair back from
her face, 'that while we're here we ought to forget the
employer-employee relationship. Think of us as just
you and me, friends, Santo and Penny, together, enjoying a well-deserved holiday.'

'And Chloe,' she amended swiftly. 'How could you
forget your daughter?' The trouble was she had liked the
way their two names had rolled off his tongue. They
sounded as good together as Tristan and Isolde, Romeo
and Juliet. Star-crossed lovers. Was that them? Were
they destined to meet only for life to thrust them apart?

'I've not forgotten her,' he said firmly, 'have no fear.
But when Chloe's in bed, when she doesn't need me,
then the only person I want is you.'

He didn't touch her but their eyes met and held and
Penny couldn't have moved if she'd wanted to. She was
gripped by something far too strong to deal with. In the
end it was Santo who turned to the ocean and looked
out.

Penny studied his profile. His thick dark hair was
swept back from a strong, proud forehead, his nose was
long and straight, his lips, those beautifully sculpted, in-
finitely kissable lips, were slightly apart, his chin was firm
and jutted only slightly. It was a strong face with silky
brows over dark, unreadable eyes, eyes that had the power
to melt her bones and make her into someone she wasn't.

And that someone was hungry for another kiss. This wasn't the sensible Penny, this was her wanton alter ego. She had become two persons since meeting Santo and she wasn't sure that she liked the side of her who had fallen under his spell. Yes, it was exciting, it was the most exciting thing that had ever happened to her. But it was something that couldn't last and was therefore wrong.

'I don't think we should stay out long,' she said quietly.

'Because you're afraid?'

Yes! Very much so, yes. But she reigned in illicit thoughts and smiled brightly. 'I have nothing to be afraid of. But I'm neglecting my duty.'

'Chloe's still asleep,' he reminded her.

'You cannot know that. How will she feel if she wakes and finds only strangers?' And how will I feel if I allow myself to have a full-blown affair with my employer?

The question was answered immediately. She would hate herself. It would be totally unprofessional.

'If you are so worried then feel free to go back up,' he answered. 'I intend staying here for a while.' He turned to look at the cliff face. 'There are steps over there. One hundred and sixty-two of them to be precise. There is a hand rail but do be careful.'

To Santo's dismay Penny walked away without another word. He had thought she would balk at the thought of all those steps, and he had known she wouldn't take the lift on her own. He wanted her, he needed her; he couldn't get enough of her.

Earlier in the lift she had returned his kiss as though she'd needed it as badly as he did. He'd soared with the angels. Not that he intended embarking on a serious relationship. He couldn't offer her that. But having Penny share his life and his bed for however long a period it took for him to get her out of his system felt like heaven.

And now she was walking away from him, giving him a clear indication that she had no intention of indulging in an affair. She had kissed him because she couldn't help herself but she didn't want to take it any further.

Except that she'd done it before!

So there could be another time!

He smiled and watched until she disappeared from sight. Then he turned back to contemplate the warm, translucent water that circled his feet, and on an impulse he stripped off his clothes and waded out until it was deep enough to swim.

By the time Penny reached the top she longed for nothing more than a long cold drink and somewhere to sit. But it wasn't to be because Chloe came running towards her. Isabella was hovering a few steps away. 'I was looking for you,' Chloe said. 'Where's my daddy?'

Pleased that Chloe seemed to be happier with her relationship with her father, Penny stooped down to her level. 'He's on the beach, my darling. I've just been there, but it's a long, long way down.'

'Can we go?' asked Chloe excitedly.

'Another time, I need to sit down for a while,' answered Penny. 'It was a big climb up and my legs are very tired.'

'But I want my daddy.'

'And I'm sure that if he knew you were awake he'd have come back up too. He won't be long, I promise.'

But Santo was much longer than Penny had anticipated and by the time he did arrive Chloe was in tears.

Afterwards, when he'd consoled her and she'd finally run away for something to drink, Penny said,

'She was waiting ages for you. What were you doing?' Though actually she didn't need to ask; his hair was wet and his feet still bare and it was obvious he'd been swimming. As she could have done if she'd stayed! The sea had been so inviting, so gloriously warm and clear.

'I didn't think she'd be awake yet.'

'That's the trouble, you never think,' she retorted, and went in search of Chloe.

It was late evening before Penny saw Santo again. She'd spent time playing with Chloe while he disappeared somewhere in the villa's interior. He reappeared when Chloe was being put to bed and insisted on reading her a bedtime story.

He'd certainly made strides in his relationship with his daughter, but to Penny it was still not enough. This holiday was supposed to be about him and Chloe spending time together and getting to know each other better—not about Santo trying to persuade his daughter's nanny to have an affair!

She was determined not to let him kiss her again. Things had gone far enough—too far, in fact. She had foolishly given him encouragement and it was asking for trouble. From now on she would remain entirely vigilant; under no circumstances would she allow him through her defences.

And who was she trying to kid?

It would be practically impossible.

However, for the next few days Santo turned his attention to entertaining Chloe; they went swimming together—the girl was a good swimmer for her age, totally fearless in the water—and they played all sorts of silly games. It did Penny's heart good to see Santo letting his hair down and Chloe so at ease in his company.

Chloe clearly no longer thought that her daddy didn't love her. She was forever flinging her arms around his neck and kissing him. At first Santo had looked a shade uncomfortable from so much affection but it wasn't long before he was kissing her back and telling her how much he loved her.

Just occasionally Chloe would ask how her mother in heaven was, and the first time Penny had held her breath as she had waited to hear what Santo would say. But he told her that she was watching over them all the time, that she saw everything they did, and wished with all her heart that she could be with them now.

It was when Chloe was in bed that Penny and Santo spent time together, dining outside usually, the cooler evening air very welcome after the heat of the day. Sometimes he'd be called to the telephone and never return. At others Penny would hurry away to her own room before anything intimate could develop between them.

She was aware of Santo's disappointment but it worried her how close they were getting. She didn't want to be hurt again and the only way she could prevent that happening was by keeping him at arm's length. And it worked until the night he told her he was taking her out to dinner.

'We can't leave Chloe,' she protested. 'What are you thinking?'

'Isabella will be on hand in case she wakes. It is time for you and me to enjoy ourselves.'

You and me! He made them sound as if they were already a twosome. Panic rose in her throat. 'I can't,' she declared, and heard the fear in her voice. Oh, heavens, she mustn't let him think that she was afraid of him, or know of the feelings he managed to evoke. 'It wouldn't be right,' she added defensively.

'So you keep saying.' A frown dragged silky black brows together, lowering them over eyes that were dark with anger. 'Forget whatever it is that's troubling you. You're joining me. I've been patient long enough.'

'Since you put it so delicately, how can I refuse?' Whether he heard the sarcasm she couldn't be sure.

He didn't smile, he simply inclined his head. 'We're leaving in half an hour.' And he stalked away.

What would he do if she dared to ignore his request? Would he drag her out screaming? Or would he go anyway—and find another woman to keep him company? This last thought sent Penny scurrying to her room.

But what to wear? She didn't even know where they were going. Undoubtedly it would be somewhere expensive, and she didn't have one suitable dress in her wardrobe. What she did have was a black camisole and a long, floaty black skirt, normally worn separately but together, with a silver belt and her silver sandals, they should meet with his approval.

She brushed her hair back, fixing it loosely in her nape with a silver clip, and after applying a stroke of mascara, a smudge of eye-shadow and a touch of lip gloss she was ready. She found Santo waiting on the terrace and when he turned to look at her Penny's breath caught in her throat.

He wore an ivory jacket over a black shirt and trousers. She had never seen a man look so amazingly handsome, so devastatingly sexy. Her heart beat so strongly it felt as though it would burst out of her chest. She didn't want to go out—she wanted to go to bed with him! Now! Forget the clothes— rip them off; let him seduce her, let them make love all night long.

But outwardly she was serene, smiling faintly.

He studied her too, his incredible brown eyes taking in every detail.

'Will I do?' she asked softly, horrified to hear how husky her voice had suddenly gone.

'You look stunning.'

No man had ever said that to her before. A fresh river of sensation danced through her, making her want to twirl and display herself for his benefit. She felt good in her own skin, more beautiful than she had ever thought she could be.

'We should be going.' His voice had deepened too, gone even lower than normal, triggering a fresh surge of awareness. And she knew, before they'd even begun their evening, that danger was in the air. It was all around her, teasing, tormenting; washing over her in unstoppable waves.

Santo wondered whether he'd made the right decision in deciding to take Penny out. He'd told himself that it was because she deserved more than to be constantly in charge of his daughter. But was that the real reason? Wasn't it himself he was thinking of?

He was the one who wanted escapism. Much as he was enjoying getting to know Chloe, much as he lapped up the love she was now unconditionally giving him, he needed something more.

And that something was Penny.

He needed exclusive female company. He had sworn to himself that he would remain the perfect gentleman, but seeing her now, he wasn't sure whether he'd be able to do that. She was beautiful in black, it suited her

English rose complexion, and with her amazing blonde hair taken back from her face she looked so young and innocent, so tempting in every way, that he knew he was lost.

Leading her outside to a waiting car, Santo wanted to take her elbow, but he knew even that small courtesy would trigger an unstoppable desire to kiss her, to hold her against him and smell the sweet, fresh scent of her skin. And from there it would be a simple step to saying to hell with the evening, let's go to bed.

And so he didn't touch her, he didn't even speak, he simply opened the car door for her, settling her in before walking round to the other side.

'A new car?' she asked with a slight lift of one fine brow as he slid in beside her.

'You don't like?'

'I do,' she admitted, 'but I assumed you were always chauffeured.'

'It depends on where I'm going and who I'm with.' He hadn't wanted a third party getting in the way tonight. 'You needn't fear for your safety, I have no intention of drinking too much.' He wanted to remember every tiny detail about this evening. He wanted it to be romantic and perfect. And hopefully by the end of it she would agree to sleep with him.

That one night she'd spent in his bed lived in his mind. He had recreated it time and time again. He had discovered a side to Penny that she rarely showed and he wanted it again. There'd been glimpses of it since but that was all. Always she withdrew back into the safety of the cocoon she'd wrapped around herself.

He was taking her to a restaurant that belonged to someone he knew. It was built into the cliff face and the views were awesome; if they were lucky they would catch a spectacular sunset. Penny couldn't fail to be moved by it.

She was silent on the way and he wondered what she was thinking. She didn't really want to be out with him, that was for sure. 'Forgive me if you feel I've bullied you into this,' he said, slanting a glance in her direction, 'but I'm sure you'll enjoy it.'

'I'm sure I will,' she answered, and her tone was so cool that he wanted to stop the car right where he was and kiss her until fire ran through her blood, until she could no longer control herself.

But of course he didn't. He would play it her way—for now. 'The restaurant isn't too far away.'

No answer.

'Are you hungry?'

A shrug of her shoulders.

'The food is superb. You do like authentic Italian food?'

'Sometimes.'

He was beginning to lose patience. 'And would to-night be one of those times?'

She turned her head finally and looked at him. 'Santo, I am here under sufferance. How do I know what I will like until I see the menu?'

Santo gripped the wheel until his knuckles whitened and hung on to his temper—just. 'I'm sorry you feel like this. Maybe I will turn the car around and take you home. Then I will come out again and dine on my own. But I tell you, you will be missing a treat.'

Penny finally relented. What was the point in antagonising Santo any further? He had taken so much trouble to arrange this evening and she was behaving like a spoilt child. In truth she was afraid. So very afraid.

Already her hormones were creating havoc. In the close confines of the car, with his hand only inches from hers whenever he changed gear, he filled every one of her five senses.

Sight. She was afraid to look at him because he had never seemed more broodingly Latin and electrifying than he did at this moment. Every inch of him excited her.

Smell. He had a special scent that was his alone. Not just his cologne, tantalising though that was, but a clean male smell that would for ever remind her of him.

Hearing. That incredible deep voice that shivered through her veins and damaged her nerve-ends. Rich and baritone, so sexy that she could listen to it for ever. So sexy that she went weak at the knees every time he spoke.

Touch. His hands on her body the night they had made love. Expert, gentle, tormenting. Stroking her into life, encouraging, arousing. Finding sensitive areas she hadn't known existed.

Taste. The taste of his mouth on hers, always clean and fresh. The taste of his skin as she had nibbled her way over it. A male taste. A taste exclusive to Santo.

And she wanted to taste him now, this very minute. She wanted to take his hand and press it to her lips. She wanted to kiss his fingers, suck them into her mouth; create fresh fantasies.

Dared she do it?

CHAPTER EIGHT

'IT'S WONDERFUL! It's totally amazing! It's out of this world!' Penny couldn't find enough superlatives to describe her first impressions. When they entered via the main door it had seemed like any other Italian restaurant. It was not until they were led through that it took her breath away.

They were on a balcony jutting out of the cliff face—practically suspended in mid-air. Leaning over the pretty white railing, she could see a village far below on the shoreline. And either side of them, nestling into the cliffs, were a few elegant villas. Santo pointed along the coastline. 'Just around that headland is where we are staying.'

Penny wished he wouldn't stand so close. His hand was on her shoulder and the heat of him, his individual male scent, was far too invasive for comfort. She turned away, missing the disappointment in his eyes.

She hadn't dared take his hand earlier for fear of showing him how desperately she wanted him, then their passion would have overtaken them and they wouldn't have made it here. It was essential that she keep everything light-hearted; getting drawn into a relationship could only spell unhappiness.

A hovering waiter pulled out a chair for her at a table far enough away from the other diners to give them a degree of privacy. And when Santo said something to him in Italian he inclined his head and disappeared.

'Santo!' A small, slim man suddenly beamed his way towards them. 'Long time no see, my friend.' The two men shook hands and clapped each other's backs.

'Now you must introduce me to this beautiful young lady. An English rose, no less. Who is she? What does she mean to you?'

Santo grinned. 'Too many questions. This is Penny. Penny, meet an old friend of mine, Enrico. We went to school together but rarely see each other these days.'

'Because you insist on living in England,' countered the other man, kissing Penny on both cheeks as she got to her feet. 'Can you understand him,' he asked her, 'when we have such beauty here?'

'England is beautiful too,' she declared. 'Have you ever been there?'

Enrico shrugged and shook his head. 'Sadly no. I do not have time. I run my restaurant, I have a large family. It is—' he held out his hands '—all I want. I am a happy man. I want for you two to be happy too.' He looked at them both questioningly.

Penny wanted to say that she was not Santo's girl-friend but Santo forestalled her.

'We are—new friends, Enrico. We are just getting to know each other.'

'Ah!' The Italian nodded knowingly. 'I leave you, then. *Buon appetito*.'

Once he had gone Penny glared indignantly. 'You let him think that we—'

'It is best,' cut in Santo. 'Enrico is an incurable romantic. He loves love. He will be happy.'

Penny wanted to protest that she was not happy about the deception—except that she knew it would do no harm. She was overreacting; they were not likely to see Enrico again. So she lifted her shoulders and then the waiter returned.

As they sipped their drinks and waited for their meal the sun, in all its golden glory, sank lower and lower in the sky until it finally disappeared. There followed a pictorial display of colours that took Penny's breath away It was an extravaganza *extraordinaire*.

She had always enjoyed the aftermath of a sunset and was not disappointed. The sky was streaked with every colour imaginable, oranges and reds, purples and blues, all reflected in the almost still waters of the sea. There were oohs and ahs all around them. And her eyes were shining as she looked at Santo.

She was surprised to find that he was watching her instead. 'Wasn't that out of this world?' she asked with a great big smile on her face, trying not to show that the way his eyes were claiming hers triggered an immediate response.

'We were lucky.'

'It was incredible.'

'I'm glad you enjoyed it.'

Polite conversation, but Penny was well aware that they could have watched this same sunset from the villa and she wouldn't have felt the same. It was special here. There was a whole different atmosphere. Each of the tables were occupied by couples, all intent on each other, all watching the sunset and then turning to their partners and holding hands across the table and kissing.

As she wanted to kiss Santo! As she wanted him to kiss her!

The spectacular solar display had generated a response that craved fulfilment. Disastrously she was falling in love with Santo. But he didn't want love, he didn't want a serious relationship, and under those circumstances it would be impossible to continue working for him. She felt quite ill at the thought that it might become necessary to hand in her notice.

Actually Santo was the man of her dreams, as far removed from Max as it was possible to be. He made her feel good about herself, all woman, sexy and beautiful, and she wanted to spend the rest of her life with him. It wasn't possible, of course. He'd made it very clear that he never intended marrying again. Love didn't enter the equation. Not as far as he was concerned anyway. And if she wasn't in love with him now she soon would be.

Their first course arrived and as darkness surrounded them candles were lit on the tables and the atmosphere heightened. It was difficult not to give in to temptation, let herself be swept along by the tide. Santo's eyes were ever-watchful on hers; he saw the mixture of emotions she was putting herself through. And if he ever found out exactly how she felt he would take advantage and it would be her undoing.

The risotto was followed by roast sea bass, then later ice cream. Santo chose a Soave to drink with their main course, though, true to his promise, he limited himself to one glass.

There was a hint of dark shadow on his strong jaw and a proud tilt to his head. It was almost the face of an aristocrat. But his eyes, those incredible, velvety dark eyes that if he so wished could melt her bones in a second, gave nothing away.

Santo hated to admit, even to himself, that Penny was getting through to him the way no one had since his wife walked out. She was as different from Helena as it was possible for a woman to be. She was caring and thoughtful—and concerned not only for Chloe's well-being, but his own as well. She was one in a million. Despite this fact, though, he was still wary of letting anything serious develop between them. He couldn't afford another mistake.

So what was he doing leaning towards her, lifting her chin with one finger, allowing his eyes to blaze into hers as his lips found their target?

As soon as he tasted her all hell broke loose inside him. This had been the real purpose behind their evening. He had been almost certain there would be a spectacular sunset and he had known that it would excite her and hopefully entice her into responding to him.

Her lips quivered beneath his, he felt her soft sigh, he tasted her sweetness and he deepened the kiss, groaning low down in his throat as he did so. His other hand slid behind the back of her head, securing her, making sure she couldn't escape. Except that delightfully she didn't want to. She returned his kiss with a passion that excited him.

He traced the outline of her face, he trailed fingers down the line of her throat, exploring the throbbing pulse before continuing his journey. Her camisole was made of some soft, silky material and he could feel her breasts rising and falling beneath it, his suspicion that she was not wearing a bra proving to be true.

'Let's get away from this place.' The growl came from deep in his throat.

And so that Penny wouldn't have the opportunity to change her mind, once they were in the car he took her hand and placed it on his thigh, keeping his own over it except for when he needed to change gear. He couldn't be sure, but he thought her fingers were creeping slowly towards the part of his anatomy that was on high alert.

If they touched it would be his undoing. 'Save me,' he whispered.

Penny chuckled and it was the most beautiful sound he had ever heard. 'From whom—yourself?' she teased.

He muttered something in Italian, his voice thick and incredibly seductive, renewing the urgent need that was building inside her. Without a word being spoken Penny knew that she was going to spend the rest of this evening in Santo's bed. And, safe in that knowledge, everything she had been thinking earlier forgotten, she took delight in tormenting him, in increasing his hunger, making it almost impossible for him to hold back.

She wanted him to make love to her, splendidly and heart-stoppingly. All night long. She wanted memories to carry with her for the rest of her life. Santo had known what he was doing when he'd taken her to that particular restaurant; he'd known that it would appeal to the sensitive, romantic side of her. And how! She was his for the taking.

Just one tiny part of her brain sent out warning signals but she ignored it. Her body ached to be possessed, she wanted to feel Santo's hands exploring and discovering all her intimate spots, inciting deeper hunger, making her writhe and twist beneath him.

Even thinking about it created fresh shivers of need and she leaned across and impulsively kissed his cheek.

Santo groaned. '*Mio Dio!* Do you know what you're doing? We'll have an accident if you're not careful.'

Reluctantly Penny sat back in her seat, closing her eyes, letting her mind take her wherever it wanted. Her hand remained on Santo's leg, her fingers stroked and teased and she delighted in the power she had over him. She was able to forget that he was her employer, she saw him only as a man capable of torturing her soul. Making her crave fulfilment.

They couldn't reach home quickly enough as far as she was concerned, and when Santo led her straight to his bedroom, her hand tightly enclosed in his, it confirmed that his needs were as deep as hers.

Once there, though, his urgency left him. 'The night is ours,' he said in his deeply erotic voice. 'There's no need to rush.' He wasn't touching her, he was letting his eyes do all the work. They stripped her naked, saw the way her nipples were tight and hard, the way she kept moistening her lips, the way she couldn't keep a limb still because the very heart of her ached with a need so great that it hurt, forcing her to dance on her toes.

'I want you, Santo,' she told him, her throat dry, her words husky and sexy, and just for a moment she felt embarrassed that she was giving so much of herself away.

'How much?' Deadly dark eyes burned into hers.

'Too much,' she admitted.

'Impossible.'

'Too much for my peace of mind.'

'Ah! You still think it is wrong to want to make love with your employer?'

Penny nodded, wishing he hadn't put it into words. She was so desperate for him and yet he was making it sound all wrong.

'Don't you think there's something dangerously erotic about forbidden love?'

It was the way he spoke, his thickened accent, that sent her over the edge. Forbidden? Yes! Wrong? Yes! Did she still want him? Yes! *Yes, yes, yes!*

'I like danger. I like erotic,' she declared and sashayed towards him, propriety now forgotten, raw need taking its place. She pressed her body up against his, linked her arms around his neck and, lifting her chin, she claimed his lips. She kissed him with such passion that she knew she would feel ashamed at some later date.

Santo needed no more encouragement. He clasped her head between warm firm hands, his kiss as fierce and demanding as her own, parting her lips, exploring, tasting, teasing, fuelling fires already alight.

And when his hands began an exploration of their own, when he slid down the straps of her camisole and palmed her naked breasts, when thumb and forefinger teased and tortured her sensitised nipples she threw back her head and thrust her hips against him. The strength of his arousal sent a shock wave through her, and the next second she felt herself being carried towards the bed.

By this time her mind had drifted away into a world of its own. Nothing else mattered except pleasure, except the release of feelings that threatened to explode any second.

Santo disposed of her camisole and skirt in one swift movement, his own clothes following. He pinned her to the bed with his body, his eyes blazing into hers, and Penny felt all the air rush from her. Her mouth went dry, her lips were dry, she ached for him so much that it hurt.

'Santo!' she whispered.

'Penny!' he growled.

'Daddy!'

They both stilled at the same time, listening hard, hearing it again. 'Daddy! Daddy!'

'Don't move,' he told her. 'I'll be back.'

CHAPTER NINE

PENNY couldn't lie in bed and wait for Santo to return. She scrambled into her clothes and followed him into Chloe's room, desire quickly replaced by concern. There had been real panic in the little girl's voice, but the positive thing about it was that she had called for her father. Santo had to feel good about that.

Chloe was sitting up in bed, her eyes wide and scared. Santo had her cradled against him, stroking her hair, saying something in Italian that neither of them understood. But whatever it was it seemed to have a calming effect on Chloe. Penny saw her visibly relax, her eyes returning to normal, even a faint smile turning up the corners of her mouth.

All Santo wore was a pair of boxer shorts that he'd pulled on quickly, and Penny found it profoundly moving to see Chloe held against his bare chest. He was no longer afraid of his daughter, his feelings now came naturally and there was no awkwardness. It was a scene that warmed her heart and she actually felt as though she was intruding.

But when she turned to leave Santo beckoned her towards him. 'Come and join us,' he said softly.

And so she climbed on the bed too, sitting the other side of his daughter. 'Was it a bad dream?' she asked gently.

Chloe nodded.

'But you're feeling better now?'

The girl nodded again and put an arm around each of them. 'Will you sleep with me?'

Penny looked at Santo and knew he was thinking that this wasn't how he'd envisaged spending the night. Nor had she. But Chloe needed them. It actually felt as if she was inviting Penny to take the place of her mother. She could never do that, ever, but as a stand-in, in Chloe's eyes, for tonight, Penny fitted the bill.

She smiled at Santo over his daughter's head. He rolled his eyes, but it was good-naturedly. 'I think we could do that, *mio bello*.'

Chloe smiled and wriggled back down the bed.

Penny bade goodbye to a night of passion and settled beside her.

Santo followed suit. Never in his life had he been interrupted when he was on the verge of making love. He knew that if anyone had disturbed him in the past he would have been extremely angry. Surprisingly he was merely aggravated. Penny would wait. The pleasure would be there whenever he wanted it. He was sure of that now. But his daughter was a different matter. He'd learned to love this little bundle of joy and her peace of mind was his main concern.

He drifted into sleep at his daughter's side and was shocked to find it daylight when he awoke. Penny was gone and Chloe giggled as she tickled his nose.

'You snore, Daddy.'

'I do not,' he declared strongly.

'Yes, you do, like this.' And she made a tiny sound in the back of her throat.

He tickled her then and the two of them were rolling on the bed in laughter when Penny came to find them.

'It's time you were up and dressed,' she said to Chloe.

Santo thought Penny had never looked lovelier. She had showered and changed into a short white skirt and a T-shirt. Her hair was still damp and curled in long tendrils over her pert breasts. He wanted to touch, to stroke her beautiful hair away, to reacquaint himself with this most tempting part of her body.

Tonight, he thought. Tonight he would take her to his bed and he wouldn't let her go until daybreak. Preferably he would like her in his bed now. His testosterone levels had rocketed the moment she entered the room.

Why not let Isabella see to Chloe?

He squashed the thought the moment it arose. For all these years he'd only ever had himself to think about, but there was his daughter now. He couldn't hand her over just because he wanted to make love to her nanny.

It was actually getting harder to think of Penny as Chloe's nanny. He felt that she belonged to him. Their positions had radically changed. He no longer saw her as one of his employees. She was Penny, his lover.

He'd been excited when she had lost her inhibitions last night and made a move on him. It had been unexpected and erotic and he couldn't wait to get her into his bed tonight.

'I don't want to get up yet,' said Chloe, 'I'm playing with Daddy.'

'Daddy's going to get up too,' he told her. 'But after

breakfast, if you're very good, we'll go swimming in the sea. Would you like that?'

Chloe nodded emphatically. 'Penny as well?'

'Penny too,' he agreed, looking across at her. She tried to hide the fact that she still hungered for him but he saw it and smiled, his smile widening even further when she turned away and led Chloe from the room.

It was mid-morning before they went swimming. A phone call had taken Santo away from them and they'd spent their time exploring the garden, watching a swallowtail butterfly glide from flower to flower, looking down at the turquoise waters of the Mediterranean, Chloe impatiently asking when her daddy was going to be ready.

At last he joined them and they went down in the lift to the beach. Chloe was filled with excitement and couldn't stand still for one second, but Penny noticed something different about Santo. He seemed slightly withdrawn and she wanted to ask him what his phone call had been about. It had clearly upset him. But it wasn't her place—it was probably to do with business anyway—so she did her best to ignore his mood and pretend that everything was well.

In the water Chloe was in her element and Santo was so good with her that Penny stood for long moments at a time just watching them. Whatever it was that had been bothering him earlier he had shrugged it off and made sure that his daughter enjoyed herself—for which Penny was grateful.

They spent all day playing with her and after Chloe had gone to bed they dined outside. The sun had gone down, the air was cooler and the lights on the terrace cast interesting shadows. It was a night made for lovers. As had every night been since they came out here.

'You do know that I want you in my bed tonight?' His voice was no more than a low throb, even the air seemed to be throbbing.

Penny drew in a painful breath and nodded. She knew that if she tried to speak nothing would come out except a breathy whisper. Besides, saying that she didn't want to share his bed wasn't an option. The very thought of it made her heart race, sent red-hot blood shooting through her veins, made her want to dance and sing, filling her with a longing so intense that it hurt.

'I love playing with Chloe, but a man needs more.'

His fantastic dark eyes never wavered from her face and Penny didn't want him to wait until bedtime. She wanted him now, this very minute, this very second. 'I need more too,' she declared huskily.

Whether it was the way that she said it, or the desperate plea in her eyes, but he groaned and almost knocked over the chair in his haste. Strong arms lifted her and held her close. His scent invaded her nostrils, as powerful as any drug. Santo was making her his own; she was submitting to him without sensible thought.

Santo's lovemaking was as spectacular as Penny had known it would be. They moved into a world apart from other humans, reaching heights unimaginable. Their bodies were completely attuned with one another, each knowing what the other wanted, needed…

It felt as if she had merely existed before, waiting for the right man to wake her, to release her from her inhibitions. She was alive, soaring high, reaching levels of sensuality that threatened to melt her bones.

At the back of her mind was the knowledge that it would one day inevitably end. It had to. But for the moment she preferred to forget that. She wanted only to greedily take what he offered.

They touched and tasted, they explored and enticed, they took and they gave. It was a night filled with passion. Sleep came and went. Each time they started afresh it was like being with a new man. Never had her body been used so much. Never had it enjoyed such intense pleasure, such deep fulfilment. She didn't want the night to end. But eventually she sank into a sleep so deep that it was mid-morning before she awoke.

The bed beside her was empty and as memories swiftly returned she felt embarrassed over her wanton behaviour. Santo must have thought he'd died and gone to heaven. She'd held nothing back. Her cheeks flamed and she jumped out of bed and raced for the shower.

Santo watched as Penny approached. She looked amazingly shy, her head down, her cheeks flushed, glancing at him cautiously from beneath lowered lashes. God, she was lovely. She'd been a siren in bed and now she was tempting him again. And how he needed her, there were things going on in his mind that called for distraction.

'I'm sorry, I overslept,' she said as she reached him. 'I've not seen to my duties this morning. Who got Chloe ready?'

'Why, her father, of course,' said Santo, surprising himself by how easily he had said that.

They played ball games in the pool before lunch, and later in the day, when the air had cooled a little, he suggested they go for a walk to explore the surrounding countryside.

Penny had felt all morning that Santo wasn't in the best of moods—nothing she could put her finger on, just the occasional irritation that gave him away—so she was delighted when he suggested a walk together. She imagined that he was getting fed up. That work beckoned him. Their lovemaking had helped but he wasn't used to taking this sort of holiday. Relaxing and playing with a child had certainly never been part of his lifestyle.

He probably jetted here, there and everywhere, staying in top-class hotels, having people wait on him hand and foot. Theatre visits and a round of social soirées were probably more in his line.

Actually the more she thought about her previous suggestion that they go to an English seaside town, the more she realised that he would not have not fitted in. She couldn't see him sitting on the beach building sand-castles, popping into a crowded café for lunch, or enjoying an evening meal in a local pub.

Not that she was complaining about his standards. She appreciated the places he took her to, the quality of the villa they were living in, his own private aircraft! She could most definitely get used to this kind of life-style.

On their walk they discovered a tiny village nestled into the hillside. It had a central *piazza* and a beautiful church that Penny explored on her own while Santo kept his eye on Chloe. There were children playing in the square and his daughter was quickly welcomed into their midst.

Penny was pleased that Chloe had found someone to play with and when she finished her exploration she joined Santo where he sat outside a café. He bought them each a *gelato*, and every one of the children as well. They must have thought all their birthdays had come together, mused Penny.

But he remained quiet and lost in thought and Penny couldn't sit there any longer without knowing what was wrong with him. 'Is something bothering you, Santo?' She posed the question gently, knowing it was none of her business but unable to sit and pretend that there was nothing wrong.

'Why do you ask?' His eyes were sharp and defensive as he turned to look at her, sending out a very strong message that she was out of order.

But Penny wasn't going to give in. 'Because you've gone very introspective all of a sudden.'

'And a man's not allowed to sit quietly, is that what you're saying? You're not the centre of my universe—'

'Santo! Of course not,' declared Penny immediately, her blue eyes very wide and hurt. 'I'm not thinking of myself.' Well, not much anyway, though she would have liked some of the warmth and interest she'd gotten used to. For heaven's sake, she'd spent last night in his bed—and now this! Almost ignoring her. What was she supposed to think?

'Do you think I'm not giving Chloe enough attention—is that it?'

'No, you've been wonderful with her,' she said quickly, 'she's enjoying herself. But it's clear you have something on your mind. Are you anxious to get back to work? Are you beginning to resent your time here?' Or was he regretting starting an affair with her? Afraid she might want more from him than he was prepared to give? He needn't fear, she knew exactly where she stood.

'You're way off the mark, Penny.' His dark eyes blazed into hers and he got to his feet. 'Yes, I do think about work; it's my lifeblood—why shouldn't I? But there are other things that concern me—and they're none of your damn business.'

Which put her firmly in her place! 'I'm just not used to you being this quiet,' she said softly, getting up too, facing him bravely. She wanted to reach out and touch his cheek, she wanted him to kiss her, to reassure her. She wanted to feel the bond that had been so strong between them last night.

For some reason he had erected an invisible barrier that she was not allowed to cross. She hoped, she really hoped that it was not going to last for the rest of the holiday. If so they might as well pack up and go home.

'Maybe you should get used to it,' he answered sharply. 'A man needs space for his thoughts sometimes.'

Penny drew in a deep breath and looked away. Now that there was nothing else left for them to say it had gone very quiet. Too quiet! Even the leaves on the trees had stopped rustling. To her horror she realised that all the children had disappeared.

'Where's Chloe?' she asked sharply, her heart beginning to hammer in her breast.

Santo swept his eyes over the deserted *piazza*. 'Weren't you keeping your eye on her?'

She couldn't blame him. It was her job to look after his daughter. 'Didn't you see where they went?'

'If I had I'd have called her back. It's as simple as that,' he declared cuttingly, striding around the square, peering along the streets leading off it.

Penny called her name to no avail. There was simply no one in sight, no one to ask. Her heart lurched painfully.

'We'll search each street in turn,' he declared, his voice rough with worry. 'I'll start this side, you take that.'

'There is the consolation that they're all together,' said Penny. 'She'll be perfectly safe wherever they are.'

'And how do we know that?' he barked. 'She may very well have wandered off on her own once the others got fed up of playing. She could be anywhere.'

Penny felt physically sick as they parted company. She could hear him repeatedly calling Chloe's name and then she heard him talking to someone in his native language. She looked back to see that a woman stood on one of the doorsteps.

Santo called to Penny. 'There's a group of children in the woods behind the church. I'm going to search there. You keep looking down here.'

Penny would have preferred to go with him. This was all her fault. If she hadn't started their silly conversation they would have seen which way Chloe had gone. She ran up and down the streets, calling and peering, seeing curtains pushed to one side, people staring out to see what was happening. But there was no sign of Chloe.

And then Santo came back from the woods, his face pale, his eyes haunted. 'She's not with them.'

If Penny had felt sick before she felt even worse now. Her stomach twisted into hard knots, her throat felt raw and tight. 'Are they the same children she was playing with?'

He nodded grimly.

'So where did she go when they went to the woods?'

'They assumed she'd run back to us.'

Penny's eyes were as wide as saucers. 'What do we do next?'

'Call the police,' he declared vehemently.

'Don't you think it's a little soon for that?' There was hesitation in her voice.

'Do you have a better idea?' he snapped.

'Are there any other play areas? Somewhere that might have caught her eye? Is there a swimming pool for instance? You know what she's like where water's concerned.'

'I don't think so,' he said, 'but we'll ask,' and without further ado he pounded on the nearest door.

An excited conversation followed, none of which Penny understood. But she guessed by the constant shaking of the woman's head that there was no pool in the area. She had never felt so dreadful in her whole life. She blamed herself entirely for not keeping an eye on Chloe. Tears sprang to her eyes and blurred her vision.

Then just at that moment, just as she thought that this was the worst day of her life and that she would probably lose her job, Chloe came into sight. She and another girl about the same age came strolling around the corner hand in hand.

When Chloe saw them she smiled widely and came running over. 'Daddy, I've found a new friend. Her name's Pia and she says I can come and play with her any time I like. I've been playing with her new puppy.'

Relieved that his daughter was safe and sound, Santo gathered her up in his arms. 'I've been so worried about you, Chloe. I didn't know where you were. Penny and I have looked everywhere for you. Next time,' he added sternly, 'you must come and ask me. You can't just go wandering off.'

'I'm sorry, Daddy,' Chloe said and her thumb went in her mouth.

'Just don't do it again, *mio bello*. Penny and I were very worried.' He kissed her before putting her down.

'Say goodbye to your new friend because we're going home now.'

He looked at Penny then, who had stood silently at his side while he told Chloe off. 'I shouldn't have shouted at you. I'm as much to blame.'

She nodded and turned her head away and he knew that there were tears in her eyes. Relief that Chloe was safe? Or because he'd upset her? It was the first time since he'd found out that he was a father that he'd experienced this awful feeling in the pit of his stomach. He was responsible for another little person and he'd failed her. So he'd lashed out at Penny, blaming her, when it wasn't her fault.

He'd had other things on his mind as well and he'd not been in the best of moods. Penny had been trying to help. She'd been concerned for him. And this was how he'd repaid her!

Gently he took her by the shoulders and turned her to face him. With gentle thumbs he wiped away the tears still damp on her cheeks. 'I'm sorry. It wasn't your fault. Forgive me?'

He turned his lips down at the corners and put on his most pleading face, and eventually Penny smiled and nodded. He touched a kiss to his fingers and touched them to her lips. 'Friends again?'

'Friends,' she acknowledged.

Because that was how he saw her these days. Not as Chloe's nanny, but as his friend.

That night she shared his bed again. She hadn't needed much persuading and Santo felt that their lovemaking had reached a new level. Penny gave herself to him so fully, so eagerly, with no holds barred. She was a woman in a million and he felt humble that she had come into his life.

The next day he suggested they go into Naples. 'It's perhaps not quite as delightful as Rome,' he told her with some pride, 'but you shouldn't miss it.'

Penny discovered that the old part of Naples had three parallel streets across the centre with small, narrow, interesting streets connecting them. There were street markets, there was washing strung high overhead, there was absolute chaos with pedestrians and cars and motorcycles all sharing the same space.

She loved the noise and the ready banter, even though she couldn't understand any of the language. She kept Chloe's hand held tightly in hers and the little girl looked in wonder at everything that was going on around her.

They popped their heads into a church where by contrast all was peaceful and quiet—and they took the *Funiculare Centrale*—funicular railway—to the top of a hill with fantastic views over the whole of Naples. In the distance they could see Mount Vesuvius and Santo told his daughter the story of how it had erupted nearly two thousand years ago and covered Herculaneum with mud and Pompeii in ashes. 'I'll take you to Pompeii one day when you're older,' he promised.

'To see ashes?' she asked, looking at him in surprise.

'Ah, but you see,' he explained, 'people have dug away the ashes and you can see what is left of the buildings and streets. It will be good for you to see it.'

Penny thought he was going way over the top of Chloe's head, but his daughter nodded wisely. 'Then I will enjoy it. Thank you, Daddy.'

By the time they reached home that evening Chloe was dead on her feet, and after she was bathed and tucked up in bed her eyes closed before either of them could kiss her goodnight.

'It's been a good day,' Santo said with some satisfaction.

Penny nodded. By now they had both showered and changed and were sitting outside sharing a bottle of wine. 'Tomorrow we will rest,' he said, 'and then we will go to Rome. We'll spend a few days there.'

She looked at him in some surprise. There was no pleasure on Santo's face and she knew that he was doing this for her sake. 'Are you sure?' Perhaps this was what had been on his mind yesterday.

'*Naturalmente*. You cannot leave Italy without seeing it. It is your dream, I know that, I have been selfish.'

Penny wanted to ask whether he had changed his mind about visiting his father while they were there, but wisely kept her mouth shut. Santo had become more Italian, she felt, since arriving here. He seemed at home in this environment, and she failed to understand why he had turned his back on his country. He and his father must have had a very big row. She couldn't imagine anything being serious enough for him to boycott both his parent and his place of birth. It was a bizarre state of affairs.

She would have liked to know more about his family, whether he had brothers and sisters for instance. Santo was very much a private man; it had been with reluctance that he'd told her about his wife. It was as though he compartmentalised his life, opening each door only if the necessity arose. Hoping that it wouldn't.

And as though he knew what she was thinking, and was afraid she might voice her thoughts, he turned the tables and said instead, 'Why don't you tell me about the guy who hurt you?'

Penny was reluctant to admit that she'd been taken

in by someone just like Santo. Rich, handsome, charming, a real ladies' man. And the thought struck her that she was in danger of doing so again. She was playing true to form. A cold shiver ran down her spine and she took a long swallow from her glass. The only good thing about it was that this time she knew the risk, and therefore could avoid it.

By not falling in love!

Except that she was already doing it. Or was it simply Santo's body that she enjoyed? A no-strings-attached affair, one that she could walk away from at the end of the day?

Penny didn't care to delve too deeply into her mind in case she came up with an answer that displeased her. So she swirled the last drops of her wine round the glass, watching it closely, as though it were of the utmost importance, before taking a breath and looking at Santo. 'Where shall I begin?'

'Isn't the beginning always a good place?' He picked up the bottle and refilled her glass. Then he sat back in his seat, his eyes watchful on her face.

'Before I became a nanny I had an office job. Max worked there too,' she admitted reluctantly and slowly. She didn't tell him that he was one of the bosses, and that she'd fallen for him as had plenty of others before her. Or that she'd thought he saw her in a different light. That would be far too humiliating.

'How long were you together?'

'A few months. I was deeply in love. He made me feel beautiful and special.'

'So what happened?'

'He dumped me,' she answered harshly. 'Suddenly, without any warning. Prior to that he'd told me that I was the only one. He bought me jewellery and clothes. I felt glamorous and loved and I wanted to spend the rest of my life with him.' She paused for a moment before adding bitterly, 'He went on to someone else, feeding her the same pack of lies.'

Unaware that her voice had risen, that her resentment was coming through when she'd been determined not to show any emotion, Penny was surprised when Santo declared loudly, 'I'd like to get my hands on him.'

'I was the fool,' she declared, 'for being taken in by him. It taught me a lesson—to never let myself get that close to a man again.'

They were in the same boat, thought Santo. Neither feeling they could trust. Neither wanting a serious relationship. Somewhere in the back of his mind was the faint niggle that he was already in deeper than he'd have preferred, but he ignored it. They both knew what they wanted—a relationship they could walk away from with no regrets.

At this moment Penny needed comforting. She'd opened her soul to him and now he had to make sure she was all right, that she didn't go on thinking about her disastrous affair. Actually he wanted to throttle the man who'd done this to her. She didn't deserve it.

He jumped to his feet and pulled her up too, then he held her close where he could feel the rapid beat of her heart dancing against him. She was hot and slightly breathless as though she was panicking, and Santo murmured words in Italian, stroking her hair, her sweet-scented hair, waiting for her breathing to return to normal.

'Is there anything you want?' he asked softly.

And was stunned when she said, 'I'd like you to take me to bed.'

It wasn't what he'd meant or what he'd expected, he'd always been the one to do the inviting. Nevertheless he didn't hesitate. Within the space of a heartbeat he swung her up into his arms and carried her into the villa.

CHAPTER TEN

As THEY got ready to leave for Rome, Santo couldn't help wondering whether he was doing the right thing. He actually preferred not to think about it. There were so many bitter memories inside him that he felt irritable every time they raised their ugly heads.

He'd phoned his brother earlier and had discovered that his name was never mentioned in the family home. Not once, apparently, had his father asked about him in all these years. It was as though he'd cut him out of his life altogether, as though he'd never existed, making Santo wonder whether taking Chloe to see him was the right thing to do.

But Chloe deserved to meet her grandfather. And his father should know about her. Whether it would help to heal the rift, God only knew.

Chloe had no other grandparents, his ex-wife's parents had died before she was even born. And soon she would begin questioning him and it wouldn't be nice for her to discover that he had fallen out with his father. It didn't make him a very good role model.

It was time to try and put the past behind him and move on. Penny had shown him that he could have true happiness—when he had thought it would never be possible again. She was an unbelievable woman.

Penny's eyes were wide when they reached the hotel. Despite being in the heart of the city it was surrounded by lush greenery. 'They call this part of Rome the green lung,' said Santo. 'It's actually the Villa Borghese Gardens. As far as I'm concerned it's the only place to stay.'

The hotel was out of this world but Penny was surprised to discover that Santo had booked them separate rooms. She wanted to ask why but the guarded expression in his eyes told her that bad memories were haunting him and it would be wise to hold her tongue.

Chloe was their saving grace. They couldn't keep her out of the swimming pool. It was bordered by gardens and trees and felt almost tropical, and the rest of the day was spent playing with her in the water or relaxing at its side. By evening Santo seemed a little calmer and they dined on their own private terrace. But if Penny had had any thoughts that he might change his mind and invite her into his bed she was very much mistaken.

He didn't even kiss her goodnight. He had retreated into himself, deep in thoughts that had nothing to do with her. He even retired before she did.

Penny spent most of the night lying awake, wondering what was going on in his mind. She guessed it had something to do with his father, who must surely live near by. She wondered again why Santo refused to visit the man and wished he would share it with her.

The following day they visited the Vatican City. Penny was in awe as she stood in St Peter's Square— it was a much larger area than she had imagined from seeing it on television. And as they looked up at the Basilica Chloe asked who lived there.

Santo's accent was deeper than she'd ever heard it. He was truly Italian. More gorgeous than ever. He even lapsed into his native language.

'What are you saying?' she asked. It had sounded romantic and beautiful and even though there was no smile on his face she knew that he had spoken from the heart.

'It is nothing,' he snapped.

Penny flinched. 'I'm sorry,' and devoted her attention to Chloe, who was running around chasing pigeons. She wished again that Santo would share his feelings with her. Surely they were close enough by now? Instead he was shutting her out, keeping all his unhappy thoughts to himself. If she had known how badly it would affect him returning to his home city she would never have said that she'd like to come.

His unhappiness was spoiling what could have been a very beautiful time spent together. He knew so much about Rome and its history that he would have made an excellent tour guide. Instead he said nothing. She and Chloe stood and looked and wondered and marvelled, while he remained broodingly silent.

The queues were too long to go into the Basilica itself. 'Another time,' Santo promised, though she knew he didn't mean it. There wouldn't be another time. He was here under sufferance because she had told him she had wanted to see it. And now she felt truly dreadful.

They made their way to the Trevi Fountain, where Chloe and Penny threw coins over their shoulders. 'It means we'll come back here another time,' Penny told her conspiratorially. Afterwards they rested on the Spanish Steps and from the top Penny admired the view across Rome. Then it was back to their hotel, which was surprisingly close, and by this time Santo had lapsed into complete silence.

Another night spent alone in her bed and the next morning they piled into the car again, but Santo didn't tell them where they were going this time. If anything he seemed in an even worse mood and they hadn't gone far when he pulled up outside a property with amazing views over the hills.

Penny looked at him questioningly.

'My father's house,' he said, almost under his breath.

She would have been ecstatic if Santo's attitude had been different. He was obviously not happy about being here and Penny understood that this was the reason behind his behaviour over the last few days.

'Are you sure you want to do this?' Penny asked and gently touched his arm.

Santo looked out into the distance and released a deep breath before speaking. 'Me? No, I don't want to do this, but for Chloe...I will do anything.'

Penny understood then. He was here because he felt that it was the right thing to do. Not for his own sake, but Chloe's. In one respect Penny was pleased and admired him for it, but if things didn't go well, how would it affect Chloe?

Penny wondered whether Santo had really thought this thing through and began to feel decidedly nervous. Her heart pitter-pattered as she followed him along the winding path to the house and she held Chloe's hand tightly in hers.

The little girl had no such qualms. 'Whose house is this, Daddy?' she asked curiously.

'This is where my father lives, Chloe,' answered Santo.

'You have a daddy too?' asked Chloe. 'Oh, goody, I want to see him.'

Santo felt his heart thudding loudly against his rib-cage as he waited for his knock to be answered. In fact he was praying that his father wouldn't be home. This was not going to be easy. How many years had it been since he'd last set foot in this house? Nineteen? Twenty? He might not even get invited in. And how would that appear in front of Penny and his daughter?

Finally the door opened and a strange woman looked at him. 'Yes?' she asked in Italian. 'What do you want?'

'Is my—is Signor De Luca at home?'

'He is. Who shall I tell him is calling?' The woman looked curiously at Penny and Chloe.

'I'll tell him myself.' Santo brushed past her and stepped inside, ignoring her startled expression. He couldn't risk his father stating that he didn't want to see him. Not now he'd come this far.

Penny and Chloe followed, Chloe's hand still held tightly in Penny's. He found his father sitting reading in the large living room. At first he was unaware of their presence and Santo was able to observe him. He was shocked by the change. His hair was white, his skin sallow, and he'd lost weight. In fact he didn't look well.

'Father,' he said in Italian.

Antonio De Luca looked up and his expression was comical, except that Santo did not smile. 'You!' the man exclaimed. 'What are you doing here?'

'I can go...' declared Santo. He should have known it was a waste of time. There was no welcoming greet-ing, even after all these years. Not a smile. No pleasure on the old man's face. 'I thought you might have had a change of heart in your old age and been pleased to see me. My mistake.' And he spun on his heel.

There was real alarm in Penny's eyes and he wished now that he'd not brought her or Chloe with him. This was something he should have done alone, tested the waters before he introduced them.

'Wait!'

Very slowly Santo turned. He found himself looking into a pair of eyes that were identical to his own. Funny, he'd not noticed it before. He'd always thought his father's eyes were hard and cold; he'd never really looked at their shape or colour. Now he saw that they were the same shade of brown, and the same thick eye-lashes fringed them. It was almost like looking into the mirror he used each morning as he shaved.

'You simply wanted to find out whether I was dead or alive, is that it?' sneered the old man, his lip curling derisively, his eyes flaming into life. 'So now you know. Satisfied?'

This was everything and more than Santo had feared. There was no welcome for him in this house. There never would be, even when his father was on his death-bed. The old man had cast him out of his life, disowned him; couldn't care less about him.

But before he could turn round again and usher Penny and Chloe outside his father spoke again. 'Who is this you've brought with you?'

Santo closed his eyes briefly, wishing he didn't have to explain, not now. Coming here had been a big mistake. He drew in a deep breath and held his hand out to Chloe. 'This is my daughter. Chloe, meet your grandfather.'

For several long seconds the only sounds Santo heard were the somnolent ticking of a clock and his own heart beating. Chloe gripped his fingers hard and stuck her thumb in her mouth. It was like a scene out of a play when someone had forgotten their lines.

Antonio De Luca's harsh words had scared Chloe and all she could do was stand and stare. Santo smiled at her reassuringly and picked her up. 'It's all right, *mio bello*,' he whispered.

She flung her arms around his neck and turned her back on the older man, looking at Penny instead over her father's shoulder.

'I have a granddaughter I know nothing about?' roared Antonio, clearly shocked. 'May the devil take your soul, Santo.' And then in English, 'And this is your wife, I presume. You never even thought to tell me that you were married.' His voice was thickly accented but perfectly understandable.

'Actually this is Chloe's nanny,' declared Santo harshly. 'My wife died. And I can see now that it was a bad idea coming here. I wish I hadn't bothered. We will leave you in peace. Come,' he said to Penny, both his voice and his face dark with anger.

'Wait!' declared the older man. 'Don't go....please. It has been a long time... Join me for dinner tonight.'

Penny held her breath as she waited for Santo's answer. She was annoyed that he clearly hadn't warned his father that they were coming, and even more exasperated that he'd not told her what he'd planned to do. Not for her own sake but for Chloe's. The girl was clearly upset. Antonio De Luca was nothing like a child's idea of a grandfather.

Grandfathers were gentle and loving and fun. This man was harshly forbidding. He was enough to frighten an adult, let alone a child.

'Impossible!' Santo's eyes were hard as he looked at his father. 'Chloe goes to bed early. I cannot leave her at the hotel.'

Antonio's eyes swivelled towards Penny and she realised that he expected her to stay with Chloe. Which was only right, considering her position. Except that she found it hard to think of herself as just a nanny these days. And she didn't think that Santo saw her in that light either—not any more. Was she wrong? Was he just playing with her? Or was the introduction purely for his father's benefit?

Despite the fact that they were lovers he had never once said that he loved her. Which could mean, she guessed, that nothing would ever come of their relationship. Which she should have known, of course. Perhaps she did. Perhaps it was wishful thinking that it was getting more serious.

She hadn't wanted seriousness. Not ever again. So why was she feeling a little miffed that Santo had introduced her as Chloe's nanny?

'Nor would I dream of leaving Penny and Chloe on their own in a strange country,' declared Santo firmly.

'Then you shall all stay here,' declared the older man. 'The matter's settled.'

There was such clear enmity between them, thought Penny, that surely Santo would find it impossible to accept his father's offer.

Two pair of brown eyes clashed and held. Both men were as strong as the other. The silence was broken by Chloe turning her head and looking shyly at the older man, slowly her thumb came out of her mouth. 'Are you really my grandfather?' And then it shot back in again.

Antonio nodded gravely. 'Yes, my child. I am your grandfather.'

Moving slightly so that she could see Santo's face Penny knew the exact second he decided to agree to his father's suggestion. A strange sort of resignation crossed it, and some of the harsh lines disappeared. Chloe had made up his mind for him. 'Very well,' he announced gruffly. 'We'll stay. I'll fetch our cases from the hotel.'

'Thank you,' said Antonio quietly.

As soon as they'd walked back out to the car Penny spoke to Santo. 'Why didn't you tell me we were coming here?'

'Because it's none of your business.' His dark eyes flared into hers and a muscle worked furiously in his jaw. His whole body was so tense that it looked as though it might snap in two at the lightest touch.

'But you don't really want to stay, do you?' she asked, adding more quietly, 'And don't you think Chloe will pick up on the tension between you and your father?'

'You have no idea why I'm doing it,' he snarled as they jumped in the car and headed for the hotel.

Once they were back and their bags unpacked Santo took Chloe out to the swimming pool. Penny followed slowly because there was nothing else for her to do. She couldn't sit in her room and she didn't fancy facing Santo's father. Besides, Santo wouldn't approve of her chatting to him, he'd made her position very clear.

She guessed that their brief affair was now over and felt sad because this holiday had been her idea. Conversely it had now ruined their relationship.

Penny swam a few lengths and then hauled herself

out, dropping onto a lounger near to Santo. 'Why do you think your father asked you to stay?' she asked hesitantly.

'Because the old dog wants to get to know Chloe,' he growled. 'It's certainly not for my sake. My brother, Vittorio, and his wife, Rosetta, have no children yet. He wants a grandchild to spoil before he dies.'

Penny was interested to hear that he had a brother. Finding out anything about Santo's family was like extracting teeth with a tooth pick.

'He likes little children,' Santo added with a harsh laugh. 'He was always good to us when we were Chloe's age because children do as they're told. It's when they get older and he can't control their minds that he finds it hard; that's when the bullying begins...'

Penny was saddened to hear this. Life was so short, why make it unhappy? What was wrong with the old man that he'd treated his family like this? Her mother had been so wonderfully kind and supportive over the years that Penny had assumed all parents were the same. 'Do you think Chloe will like him?'

'Once she gets over her shyness. Actually, look at her...' They both turned their heads and watched Chloe slowly making her way towards the house. The thumb was in her mouth but she didn't falter. 'She kept asking me if he really was her grandfather. She's intrigued. She wants to talk to him even though she's a little afraid.'

'Should I go with her?' asked Penny.

Santo swiftly shook his head. 'She'll be safe with my father. I loved him too when I was her age.'

Penny sighed. 'It's a shame things change. And I truly never realised how traumatic it would be for you coming here.'

'I always swore I never would.'

'But you put Chloe's needs before your own?'

Something shifted in his eyes and he turned his head away. And before she knew it he'd dived back into the pool. Penny watched his long lazy strokes for a few seconds and then turned to see where Chloe was—just in time to see her entering the house through the terrace doors.

They led into Antonio's living room so she strained her ears in an effort to listen to their conversation—but she was too far away. She knew Chloe well enough, though, to realise that if the girl wasn't happy she'd come running back out.

'Why don't you join me?' Santo halted in front of her, shaking the water from his hair and eyes.

Penny wanted to swim with him more than anything. She longed to slide her body against his, to tease him, to have him grab hold of her and kiss her. Even thinking about it caused a serious disturbance in the pit of her stomach. But she remembered the way he had introduced her. 'It's not proper for a nanny to swim with her employer,' she protested, lifting her chin and trying to look outraged.

'*Touché*,' he agreed, 'but what did you expect me to tell my father? He's a stickler for propriety.'

'And if he saw us swimming together he'd have a fit, is that it? I have no wish to cause any more friction between you. Although—' she said with her fingers mentally crossed '—I would like to know why you fell out. It might help me understand your situation better.'

Santo drew in a harsh, ragged breath and his eyes flashed fierce unhappiness. Penny thought he was going to tell her that it was no business of hers, but after a few anxious moments he hauled himself out and sat on the edge of his sun lounger, facing her.

Long seconds passed. Water dripped from his hair down his face, pausing on his beautiful, long eyelashes, glistening like diamonds. It ran in rivulets down his chest and she wanted to touch, she wanted to trace each line with gentle fingertips. What she really wanted to do was arouse him, set fire to those strong male hormones and enjoy lovemaking right here in the sunshine.

She didn't like seeing him unhappy. He needed to lay his ghosts, yes, but she'd never dreamt that it would be this hard. And she wanted to do something to ease the situation. But how could she if she didn't know all the facts?

Finally he spoke. 'My father wanted to control my life. I would not allow it. It's as simple as that.'

'Is anything that simple?' she asked, thinking about her relationship with Max. That had seemed simple in the beginning. She had grown up a lot since then. 'How did he want to control it?'

Santo's eyes grew as hard as bullets. 'I can see you won't rest until I tell you.'

Penny nodded briefly. It would probably have been for the best if she'd suggested they forget it. But there might not be another occasion to ask these questions and she really did want to know what was behind his falling out with his parent.

'My father is a control freak.' A long sigh followed, together with a few moments silence. Penny could see his mind going back over the years. 'He manipulated everyone, including my mother. I don't know why she put up with him for so long. Actually, yes, I do. She did it for our sake. Mine and my brother's. As soon as

Vittorio and I were of an age when we no longer depended on her, my mother left. She returned to her beloved England. She had never been truly happy in Rome.'

Santo closed his eyes for a few seconds and Penny knew he was reliving that scene. Her heart went out to him and she wanted to throw her arms around him, make him feel better—but remembered in time that his father might be able to see them.

'My father was furious, I have never seen anyone before or since in such a rage. I could not stay there or I would have hit him. I decided to join my mother.'

'And your brother, what did he do?' she enquired softly, hating to see the look of pain in his eyes.

'He stayed. He's weak. He let my father walk all over him,'

'Do you have contact with your brother?'

Santo nodded. 'I phone him occasionally. Vittorio and his wife actually lived with my father for the first few years of their married life until he finally plucked up the courage to leave. The old man doesn't deserve loyalty. He didn't even attend my mother's funeral.'

It was a sad story and compulsively Penny reached out. 'I'm sorry.'

Santo held her hand tightly between both of his. She saw the hurt and sadness behind his eyes and wished there was something that she could say or do to make him feel better.

'What does your father know about your—personal circumstances?' She posed the question carefully, fearing that she might be going too far again.

'Nothing.'

'Not that you're a very successful businessman?'

'Let's say I have not told him,' declared Santo tersely.

'But since you're world-renowned it's a possibility?'

'I guess so.'

'And you've not been in touch since the day you walked out?'

'I've tried,' he answered, his eyes flashing with fresh anger. 'But not once would he take my call, not even when my mother died. And if it hadn't been for you I wouldn't be here now.'

'I'm sorry,' she said quietly.

'Don't be; it's probably for the best,' he said, letting go of her hand and standing up. 'I have to be the best father I can be to Chloe—you taught me that. Chloe needed to know that she has a grandfather. And by the time she's grown up, well, I guess he'll no longer be around, so she'll never see the harsh side of him. She'll have happy memories. Come and join me for a swim.'

And this time Penny didn't refuse.

CHAPTER ELEVEN

IN HEIGHT, Santo's brother, Vittorio, was the same as Santo, but otherwise they were as different as it was possible for two brothers to be. Whereas Santo's face was all hard angles and his body perfectly honed, Vittorio was fleshy around his jowls, suggesting that he liked his food too much—and consequently he carried more weight.

But it was in his manner where their differences were most apparent. Vittorio was loud and didn't care what he said, and he was hurt that Santo had never let him know that he had a daughter.

'Why did you not tell me?' he asked petulantly, like a child quizzing his parent.

They were seated at the dinner table in a room overlooking the hills leading to Rome. Santo sat at Penny's side and his brother was directly opposite her.

She felt Santo stiffen and when she darted a glance at him his face was totally impassive. 'Do you think that I'm proud of the fact that my child didn't even know she had a father? Or that I knew nothing about her? Why would I want to sing it from the rooftops? It's hard enough to bear as it is.'

'What did you do to Helena to make her hide her daughter away like that?'

Santo drew in a deep breath and paused a long moment before answering quietly, 'I didn't need to do anything. Helena was a law unto herself.'

'I always wondered why she left you.'

'And you'll have to go on wondering,' returned Santo evenly. 'I do not discuss my private life with anyone— not even my brother.'

Penny admired his self-control but Vittorio wasn't finished. 'It seems to me that you have something to hide. All this secrecy.'

'And you, dear brother, would do as well to keep your mouth shut or I won't answer for the consequences.' Santo's eyes blazed with fury; he was unable to keep his emotions in check any longer.

'He's right, darling.' Rosetta, beautiful Rosetta with her scarlet lipstick and nail polish to match, and her heavily made-up eyes, tapped her husband on the arm. 'I'm sure Santo will tell you when he's good and ready.'

'Which will be never,' snapped Santo, his eyes daring Vittorio to say anything more.

All their father did was sit at the head of the table and watch the drama unfold. He was enjoying it, realised Penny, but she wasn't. Even though she knew it wasn't her place to say anything—she was actually surprised that she'd been invited to dine with them at all—she knew that she had to, she hated the way Vittorio was questioning Santo.

'Tell me, Vittorio,' she said, 'what you do for a living?'

It was a perfectly ordinary question as far as she was concerned, it never occurred to her that it could inflame the situation further.

Vittorio's face went a fiery red and she thought he was going to bang his fist on the table.

'My husband's health doesn't let him work,' answered Rosetta for him, her hand on Vittorio's arm as she looked fondly into his eyes.

'In other words he's a kept man,' declared Santo. 'He's never done a decent day's work in his life. I'm surprised he ever found himself a wife.' He scraped his chair back from the table. 'I need some air.'

Penny excused herself and hurried after him, not even caring that it might seem strange. 'I wish you'd told me more about Vittorio. I've really put the cat amongst the pigeons, haven't I?'

'Why should I have said anything?' he asked harshly. 'I'm not proud of the fact that he's sponged off my father all his life and I'd like to bet he's still doing it to his wife. Rosetta works but she doesn't bring in enough to fund his lifestyle. He gambles and drinks—he's a complete waste of time. I thought marriage would change him, but he's still the same as he ever was. You can see now why I didn't want to come here. I've no love left for either my brother or my father. Thank God for you,' he groaned. 'One little bit of sanity in an insane world. I can't do without you any more. Will you stay with me tonight, Penny?'

It was a totally unexpected question here in this house where he had introduced her as Chloe's nanny. Even thinking about sharing his bed turned her bones to liquid. Santo was such a fantastic lover that she would never tire of him. It wasn't that simple, though. 'What will your father think?' she asked, hearing the unease in her voice.

'Who cares?' he demanded harshly. 'He's probably

already guessed anyway. Didn't you see the calculating way he looked at us earlier? I need you, Penny.'

But only to take his mind off his present unhappy state of affairs. Making love was a good problem-blocker but it didn't resolve it. He'd invited her into his bed before; he would very likely do it again. Was she foolish to let herself be used like this?

The answer was yes, she probably was, but how could she help herself when her body was attuned to his so closely that she sometimes felt a part of him? When his kisses rocked the heavens and even the lightest touch of his fingers sent her spinning into space?

And so in bed later Penny held nothing back. She took the lead, kneeling over him, stroking and kissing, trying to ease the tension in his limbs. Today had been so hard for Santo that she knew he wouldn't relax immediately. With fingers and tongue she explored and tasted, slowly and sensually, from his throat down to his navel, tempted to go further but knowing that it was too soon yet. She sucked and gently bit his nipples, exulting when he groaned deep in his throat, when he grew hard and excited.

She lay over him, moist and ready, and knew exactly what she was going to do—until suddenly Santo turned the tables. She was beneath him now. And he didn't waste time. He was hot inside her, fiercely demanding. Her muscles closed around him and she lifted herself up to meet his fiercely hungry demand.

Her fingernails dug into his back and she rocked with him until suddenly he lost all control. Seconds later Penny reached her own earth-shattering climax and for long moments they both lay on the bed, spent.

'You are some woman,' he said gruffly.

'I aim to please,' came her demure reply. Except that inside she felt anything but demure. Santo made her feel like a princess, beautiful and needed, and aroused emotions far deeper than she had ever thought herself capable of. When Santo made love to her it was as if she was in a different world where only senses mattered. Each time it was a different mind-blowing experience. And even though she knew he had only used her tonight, somehow it didn't matter.

When he was asleep she lay curled against him, her head nestled into his shoulder, her arm across his chest, the scent of him continuing to tantalise her nostrils. The feel of his skin beneath her fingertips made her want to trace every inch of his body, to feel again the exciting hardness of him. She wanted to be with him for ever!

It was such a crazy, impossible thought that tears squeezed from her eyes and when she finally went to sleep she dreamt that she and Santo were out walking on a cliff top that suddenly fell away beneath their feet. She managed to hold on to a small bush that had amazingly remained anchored, but Santo fell to his death. And she knew it was her subconscious preparing her for the fact that one day it would be all over between them.

She woke to find Chloe snuggled in the bed, sandwiched between her and Santo. 'I like my grandfather,' she declared, 'he's funny. What are we going to do today, Daddy? Nonno says he will swim with me. Can old men swim, Daddy?'

Santo smiled indulgently. 'Of course. My father was one of the best swimmers in Italy. He taught me to swim. But I actually wanted to show Penny some more of the sights and I was hoping you'd come with us.'

Swift tears welled in Chloe's eyes. 'But Daddy, I want to stay here. I want to swim. I don't like old buildings.'

'I'll talk to your grandfather,' he promised.

'I'm not sure it would be wise letting her stay,' said Penny, once Chloe had run out of the room. 'Your father might have been a good swimmer in his time but is he capable of looking after Chloe? What if anything happens? He's not quick any more, is he? And won't he think it strange if I go off with you?'

'I have fears too, but I didn't want to spoil Chloe's happiness. I'll talk to him.'

In the end it was decided that Signora Moretti, the housekeeper, would invite her daughter, who had a child about Chloe's age, to come and keep Chloe company. Santo and Penny waited for them to arrive and reassured themselves that Chloe would be in safe hands before departing. Chloe herself was in her element.

Even so Penny still felt faintly anxious. It didn't feel as though she was doing her job properly. Santo on the other hand didn't seem to have any such fears. 'Italians love children; nothing will happen to her. She will be treated like one of their own.'

They both lapsed into silence on the drive into Rome. Penny was getting a pretty good picture of what Santo's life had been like: a father who detached himself from his family, and a brother who was consumed by jealousy because Santo had made something of his life. She could see how this had moulded Santo into the private person that he was. And why he had found it difficult to bond with Chloe. There had been no love in his family—even his wife had walked out on him.

She had no idea what his mother had been like, but she had the feeling that she'd been sparing with her love also. It had probably been knocked out of her by her bullying husband.

She felt sorry for Santo. Not that he would appreciate sympathy. He'd become a tough, hard-working man who'd pushed everything unhappy out of his mind. He would be horrified if he knew she was thinking that she would like to spend the rest of her life making it up to him.

An impossible dream, but it was unfortunately true.

'We'll do the touristy things first and the shops later,' said Santo as soon as he'd parked.

'Shops?' queried Penny.

'Do not all women like to shop? There's everything here—Versace, Valentino, Armani.'

'And way out of my price range,' she pointed out. 'But I suppose it won't hurt to look. At least I can press my nose to the windows.'

She missed the curious look he gave her, and hummed happily to herself as they walked once again to St Peter's Square. She discovered to her surprise that Santo had arranged a private tour.

Their guide told them that the Vatican Museums were originally meant for the sole enjoyment of the pope; that there were two thousand rooms stretching over nine miles, and it would take them twelve years to look at every item.

Penny gasped and he laughed. 'Do not worry, we are just going to look at the highlights today.'

The decorations, the paintings, the statues, the ornateness of it all took Penny's breath away. She couldn't speak she was so overwhelmed. And she wished that she'd thought to bring her camera. The Sistine Chapel was stunning. She'd seen it on television but to actually be there and look up at the amazing ceiling, to wonder how anyone could paint such exquisite pictures, was beyond her.

And then the Basilica itself. There was so much marble and the size was so vast that Penny found it difficult to comprehend. 'It's claimed to be built over the tomb of St Peter,' their guide told them, 'and is the largest Catholic church in the world.'

Penny felt tiny in comparison and she took hold of Santo's hand as they looked up as if it would somehow make her feel more secure.

'You're enjoying it?' he asked softly.

'I feel totally insignificant,' she answered. 'I had no idea it was so large or so beautiful.'

Once outside again in the bright sunlight, they crossed St Peter's Square, which was now packed with people and found a small, quiet back-street café, where they had a sandwich and ice cream, and then it was on to the shops, to Via Condotti, where most of the designer boutiques were.

Santo insisted on taking her inside one of them, where she tried on a variety of dresses and skirts and fancy tops especially for his benefit. The assistants bowed and scraped, unable to take their eyes off him, almost ignoring Penny so eager were they to please him.

'So which ones are you having?' he asked finally.

Penny knew that he had to be joking. These were way out of her league. 'If I could afford any, which I can't, of course,' she said, 'I'd have the black cocktail dress, the tan skirt, and the blue one, I think, as well as that delicious little lacy top. Oh, and probably that slinky pink suit as well. I felt a million dollars in that.'

She missed the gesture Santo made to the manageress and was stunned when she came out of the dressing room and discovered that everything she had mentioned had been packed into bags and was ready to take away.

'Santo! You can't do that!' she exclaimed. 'I thought this was a game.'

'I don't play games,' he told her.

But his generosity worried her and on the way back to the house Penny continued to tell Santo off for spending so much money. 'You shouldn't have done that. It's not right,' she insisted.

'Aren't they what you wanted?' he asked.

'I love them but—'

'Then the matter's closed,' he said quietly.

It had been a perfect day, thought Penny as they pulled up outside. She'd seen so much of historic interest, so much wealth and beauty, that it still continued to awe her, and as she took her new purchases upstairs she couldn't stop smiling.

Santo had thought that spending the day with Penny, seeing her pleasure when she tried on outfit after outfit, would lift the depression that had overtaken him. But it had done no such thing. The instant he set foot in his father's house it was back again, hanging over his head like a thundercloud.

He had hoped, he had prayed even, that his father might have mellowed over the years, that he might actually have been pleased to see him. But no. There was no softening of the old man's heart. He was still very much the oppressor.

At least he hadn't hurt Chloe—in fact he'd welcomed his granddaughter; he'd given her love and affection, which should have pleased Santo— and did in a moderate sort of way. But Santo knew that beneath the surface his father hadn't changed. He enjoyed conflict, he enjoyed power over people, to such an extent that he had no friends.

It would be interesting to know what his father thought about his success. Penny was right; he probably did know—Vittorio would have told him—but not once had he mentioned it and Santo himself had no intention of saying anything. Ironically he had his father to thank, because if he hadn't left home, if he hadn't needed to support himself, he might not have got where he was today. It had been sheer drive and determination that had made him do it.

All this made Santo treasure the daughter he'd never known about. He loved her so much that it hurt. He would never treat her badly. He would love and cherish her to the end of his days.

Penny had had such a lovely day that she was disappointed when Santo changed as soon as they got home. He withdrew into himself; he didn't sit and talk to his father as any other son would have done. He wandered out into the garden instead and stood for ages looking out over the countryside. The void between them was too big to ever be bridged. A lump lodged in Penny's throat every time she thought about it.

Dinner was uncomfortable again. She did her best to break the silence, but conversation became monosyllabic and eventually she gave up. Once it was over Santo shut himself in his bedroom and she didn't dare follow.

It was all she could do to fight down tears. When she thought of all he'd spent on her, of the lovely time they'd had when she tried on the dresses and paraded and flirted in front of him, it was hard to believe that he was now letting the enmity between him and his father ruin it.

Surely he could have made an effort? Didn't he realise how awkward it was for her? How it would affect Chloe if he carried this on tomorrow? Or was he planning to go home then? She really had no idea what he was going to do. All she knew was that she'd never before found herself in such a difficult situation.

The next morning, however, the whole affair faded into insignificance. What was happening between Santo and his father was nothing compared to what was happening to her.

CHAPTER TWELVE

SHE was late! And she was never late. Her monthly cycle was as regular as clockwork.

When the appalling truth hit her Penny felt sick. In the stark light of morning she stared at her shocked face in the bathroom mirror. She looked truly awful— dark circles beneath her eyes, every trace of colour drained from her cheeks. Haunted, a picture of sheer fright. Her normally pretty blue eyes were wide and traumatised; she felt as though she would never be able to look at herself again.

When she thought back there had been only one occasion when Santo hadn't used protection—when they'd each been too desperate to even think about it.

And that was all it had taken!

One tiny mistake to ruin her whole life.

All they'd thought about was pleasuring each other's bodies, pleasuring themselves; nothing else had been in their minds. Just each other. Just the joy of giving and receiving, the intense excitement, the serious sensations that had screamed through every vein, every artery, every limb—until the ultimate release. A powerful, mind-blowing moment that had left them writhing on the bed, entirely unaware that in those few seconds a new life had been created.

She had not even thought about it since, not until she opened her diary and realised what the date was. Now she sat on the edge of the bath and dropped her head in her hands. She'd have to tell Santo, of course, it was only right that he should know. She couldn't walk out on him as his wife had done and not let him know that he had fathered another child. But she pitied the poor baby who'd be born into a family where father and grandfather were estranged, where an uncle lived on handouts from his parent. Where there was no love.

Oh, God, what a mess!

It took an effort to shower and dress and accept that she had to face Santo and pretend for the moment that nothing was wrong. She needed to be sure they were completely alone when she told him; she dared not risk being disturbed because she knew there would be tears and recrimination. Tears were close to the surface even now. She couldn't believe that she'd been such an idiot.

On the other hand, looking on the bright side, perhaps she wasn't pregnant. Perhaps she was worrying for nothing. Admittedly she was never late but then again she'd never had so much excitement in her life. This visit to Italy was one of her dreams come true, and to be treated like a princess by an exciting, gorgeous man had to have an effect on her.

And who was she trying to kid? Hadn't she felt nauseous the last few mornings? She'd put it down to a change of diet. But it was no good believing that morning sickness didn't happen until a few weeks into pregnancy because her sister had suffered the very same symptoms. Yes, she was pregnant all right.

She found Santo and Chloe on the terrace eating breakfast. Chloe was still in her pyjamas and she had jam all round her mouth. She was jigging up and down with happiness and it did Penny's heart good to see her. It worried her, though, how Santo would take the news that he was about to become a father for a second time. She didn't believe he was ready for it. He'd already had one child launched on him, interfering with his busy work schedule. How would he adapt to another?

'Ah, you're here at last,' he said, his eyes meeting hers briefly. 'Chloe's all yours now—I'm going out.'

And before she could ask him how long he would be, he'd gone.

Penny had been apprehensive about seeing him, hoping he wouldn't question her pallid skin and lack-lustre eyes, ready with the excuse that yesterday had worn her out, that it felt like an anticlimax. He'd barely glanced at her; he'd seen none of her torment.

Food was the last thing she wanted but she managed a glass of fruit juice and a bread roll before the house-keeper came to clear the table. The rest of the morning was spent entertaining Chloe. They swam, they walked, they explored, but on their own. The child was disappointed that her father had disappeared and kept asking when he would come back.

They ate lunch with Antonio and when he announced that he was going to take a siesta Penny put Chloe to bed as well. Their morning activity had worn her out— Penny too, if the truth were known.

She sat outside on the terrace. There was plenty of shade and a gentle breeze whispered through the foliage, so even though the temperature was high it didn't feel uncomfortable. She tried to read a magazine but the words merely danced in front of her eyes. There was no way she could concentrate when so much was going on in her mind.

Eventually Santo put in an appearance and she smiled tentatively. 'Where have you been?' she asked. 'Chloe missed you.'

His eyes were hard as he looked at her, his brow furrowed. She'd rarely seen him look this fierce before. Even his lips were grim—which didn't bode well for what she had to tell him.

'I had something to take care of,' he answered a little harshly. 'Where is she?'

'Asleep. Your father's taking a siesta too.'

'Good, because we need to talk.'

'I want to talk too,' she said quickly, 'there's something I have to tell you.' She needed to do it straight away, before she lost her nerve. It wasn't a particularly good time with Santo in this mood, but when would it be? She didn't want to wait…she couldn't; she couldn't bear the thought of carrying this secret around for any longer than necessary.

But Santo had other ideas. 'Whatever, it will wait,' he declared impatiently, dropping onto the chair opposite her.

Penny would have preferred him at her side, where he couldn't see her face so clearly. It would be purgatory trying to hide her emotions. 'Santo, I—'

But before she could get any further he butted in. 'Is this about Chloe?'

Penny frowned. 'No.'

'Is it about my father?'

'No.'

'Then I don't want to hear any of your problems, I

have enough of my own. Dammit, Penny, you're forgetting your position here.'

Penny felt as though he'd slapped her hard on the face. She felt as if she was an insect that had been trodden on by someone's big boot. She felt as insignificant as an ant. And without a further word she got up and ran to her room.

Santo had just made it stunningly clear that their relationship was over! And it hurt as nothing else had ever hurt in her life. What she ought to have done was stood her ground and asked him what the hell he meant instead of scuttling away like a scared child. She guessed it was her hormones playing up because normally she would have done that. She would have faced any situation. Had Santo forgotten all their time spent together? The hours in each other's arms making love? He'd needed her then; he hadn't been able to get enough of her. So what had happened to turn it around?

She wondered whether it was to do with his father. There was no sign of a reconciliation. Had Santo gone out because he couldn't bear to be in the same house? Even so, why take it out on her? What had she done? And how was she going to tell him that she was pregnant with his baby when he was in such a bad mood?

In her heart of hearts Penny knew that such a delicate subject should be discussed only when they were at ease in each other's company. Perhaps she ought to leave it until tomorrow? Or maybe she could creep into his room tonight, sneak into bed with him; use her body to coax him into a good mood. She knew exactly what it took to arouse him, to make him groan and gather her close, to make him lose himself inside her. It would be an excellent time to bare her soul.

Santo was well aware that he ought not to have spoken so harshly to Penny but, dammit, he was so filled with rage and frustration that anyone who came near him was in the firing line. He'd spent most of the morning on the phone to his London office and, boy, had they received the harsh edge of his tongue when he discovered there was a problem they'd been unable to solve.

It had been a bad idea coming here. He'd given his father one last chance and it hadn't worked. There'd been no welcome for his long-lost son, nothing but more of what he'd endured all those years ago. Antonio could go to hell now as far as he was concerned.

Of one thing he was very sure; he would never treat his daughter the way his father treated him. Not ever, not as long as he lived. He would treasure her and guide her and give her every support possible. She would grow into a beautiful, well-adapted young woman with no harsh memories of a father who didn't love her.

Tomorrow they were flying home. He was needed at the office—and would he be thankful to get away! But first, he supposed, he ought to seek Penny out and apologise. Except that in all honesty he was in no mood to do it.

He went for a swim instead, punishing himself, length after length, powering his arms through the water until he was exhausted. And it worked. Some of his bitterness and anger faded and when he saw Penny walking towards him he was ready to talk.

She'd said that she had something to tell him and he'd rudely cut her short. What if it *had* been about Chloe? Perhaps his daughter wasn't well? She was asleep apparently but she didn't always take an afternoon nap. Was there something wrong? Alarm bells began to ring in his head, especially as Penny looked pale and drawn, desperately worried about something.

He too began to feel fearful and he spoke as soon as she reached his side. 'Is Chloe all right? Is she still asleep?'

'Your daughter's fine,' Penny answered quietly.

'So what is wrong? Is it you who's not well?'

Penny closed her eyes briefly. 'I'm OK, but there is something I need to tell you. May I sit down?'

'Of course. Would you like a drink—some water perhaps? You look a little pale. Has the sun got to you?' He felt guilty now for scaring her away earlier. She had turned wide, shocked eyes on him and run like a rabbit for the safety of the house.

'Water, yes, thank you.'

Penny took a few deep, steadying breaths while Santo was away. From her bedroom window she'd seen him swimming and recognised that he was chasing his demons. He looked calmer now and she kept her fingers mentally crossed that he wouldn't slip back into his rage when he heard what she had to say.

When he returned with her drink he had donned a pair of cotton trousers and a T-shirt and he even smiled as he filled her glass from the jug. 'This heat is unforgiving, you know. You need to be careful.'

Penny drank deeply before setting the glass back down on the table. 'It's not the heat that's affecting me.'

'So what is it? The tension between me and my father? I'm sorry about that, and I've—'

'No!' declared Penny at once. And, since there was no way she could wrap up her confession in pretty words, she blurted it out. 'I'm pregnant, Santo.'

The silence that followed was unending, and deafening. Penny avoided looking at him. She didn't want to see the horror, the disbelief, the shock, the denial.

When he did finally speak there was recrimination in his voice. 'It is impossible. You are mistaken.' His accent was deep and there was nothing but harsh shadows across his face.

'No, I'm not,' she declared, trying to keep her voice level, to not let him hear any tremors. 'Believe me, I know how I feel. I'm carrying your baby.'

'But when, how?' Dark eyes were still disbelieving. 'I've always taken precautions.'

'Except once,' she reminded him firmly. 'Maybe you don't remember, but I do. Naturally, when we return to England I'll be handing in my notice. I won't deny you access to the baby, but—'

'The hell you won't!' Santo's roar rent the air. It seemed to echo around them and everything stilled. Even Penny's heart stopped beating. 'If—and I won't accept it until you've seen a gynaecologist—you are pregnant, then you're going nowhere.'

Penny's eyes flared a vivid blue. 'Do you really think I'd let a man who finds it so hard to love that he can't even make it up with his own father bring up my child? A man who spends more time at work than he does at home? Not in your wildest dreams.'

Her heart beat so fiercely that it hurt and, fearing that she had gone too far, Penny stood up with the intention of fleeing again, but Santo was having none of it. Eyes hard he unceremoniously pushed her back down. 'We haven't finished.'

An icy shiver ran down the length of Penny's spine but there was no way she was going to let him intimidate her. This was her baby—he hadn't asked for it, he didn't want it. It broke her heart to think that she had to walk away from him, but what choice was there? 'I don't think there's anything left to say.'

'You really think I'd let you go?'

'Other than locking me up, how can you stop me?' she challenged.

'You could marry me.'

Silence! Complete and utter silence. Even the birds stopped singing.

'Marry you?' she whispered eventually. 'Just because I'm carrying your baby? You really think that would work?' She shook her head. 'You're out of your mind.' And she was out of her mind because just for one crazy second she had thought about saying yes. And how stupid was that when he'd only proposed because she was pregnant? She was useful to him, yes—she was good at looking after Chloe, and she'd be good with the new baby, and she might even feed his sexual desires occasionally, but as for anything else…

Santo was definitely not marrying material. Not since his first marriage had ended in disaster. He didn't trust women, full stop. He might even believe that she'd gotten pregnant deliberately in order to trap herself a rich man.

'I'm perfectly serious,' he told her, 'and I cannot see why—'

'Daddy, Daddy, you're back.' Chloe came running out of the house and flung herself into his arms. A sigh of relief whooshed from Penny's lungs and she quietly slipped away while he was chatting to his daughter.

For the rest of the day she carefully avoided Santo. And that night over dinner with his father he announced that they were leaving early the next morning. 'I need to get back,' he announced tersely.

'Or is it that you've had enough of me?' barked the old man.

Santo glared. 'I would have thought it was the other way round. At least you've been kind to my daughter, I'm grateful to you for that.'

'And I wasn't kind to you, is that what you're claiming?' The cold glint in Antonio's eyes revealed exactly how much enmity there still was between the two men.

Penny shivered.

'Why do you think I walked away from you?' challenged Santo.

'Because you were a mummy's boy and wanted to be where she was,' sneered Antonio.

Santo shook his head. 'You're so wrong, Father. But I refuse to sit here and argue. I've finished.' And he scraped back his chair.

Penny pulled a wry face after he'd left the room. 'I need to pack, if you'll excuse me.'

He didn't try to stop her, and for a brief moment she felt sorry for Antonio. On the other hand he deserved everything he'd got. He wasn't a very nice father. There was such bitterness inside him, such anger. Penny could suddenly see that this old man had affected Santo terribly.

She couldn't marry him, she couldn't. She had to get away, away from all of this.

As she carefully packed the beautiful new clothes that Santo had bought her, she realised that soon she wouldn't be able to wear any of them. And would she want to anyway? They would for ever remind her of this disastrous holiday.

There was silence on the plane journey home. Even Chloe was silent. It was as though she'd picked up on their vibes and was afraid to speak in case she got into trouble.

And once they were cleared through the airport Santo announced that he was going straight to the office. 'There's a problem which no one seems capable of dealing with.'

A problem bigger than seeing that his precious daughter got home safely, or bigger than discussing your unborn baby? thought Penny bitterly as she climbed into the chauffeur-driven car he had provided for them.

Chloe slipped her hand into Penny's on the journey home. 'Is Daddy cross with me?'

'Of course not, my darling,' said Penny, feeling her heart lurch. 'Daddy has problems at work that he needs to sort out.'

Wide eyes were plaintive. 'Will he be home to kiss me goodnight?'

'I'm not sure,' answered Penny gently, 'but I'll be there. Don't you worry about that.'

'I miss my mommy.'

It was a cry from the heart and an ice-cold shiver slid through Penny's veins. Chloe hadn't said this since the early days of her coming to live with her father. She'd learned to trust and love him and now she felt that he was letting her down again. And if Penny gave up her job, as she desperately wanted to do, she would be letting Chloe down as well.

How could she stay, though, under the circumstances? She needed to be loved too, not be used as a bed partner whenever Santo felt like it, not just as a nanny to his daughter. She wanted more, much more. She'd fallen irreparably in love with Santo and she wanted to spend the rest of her life with him. It was an impossible dream, though.

They were both in bed when he came home. Penny heard his footsteps coming up the stairs and she held her breath, praying he wouldn't come to her and demand they finish their conversation. They needed to talk, yes, they needed to sort things out, but she wanted to wait until he'd had time to calm down, accustom himself to the situation.

She worried for nothing and the next morning he left before she and Chloe had breakfast. They went for a walk, took bread to feed the ducks on the river, and on the way back Penny popped into a chemist and bought a pregnancy-testing kit. Not that she needed proof, not in her own mind, but Santo did and she'd be happy to provide it. She wasn't going to see one of his fancy gynaecologists, that was for sure. She'd see her own doctor.

The only problem about leaving Santo was where was she going to live. She'd shared a flat with a friend at one time, but there wasn't room for her now. She could, she supposed, lodge with her sister for a while, she didn't have much room since they'd had the new baby, but she'd make do.

The test proved positive and although she had known that it would, it was still a shock to her system and she broke down in tears. Nevertheless when Santo came home early, she had herself well under control.

Chloe was delighted to see her father and Penny was pleasantly surprised when he supervised her bath and put her to bed. Once she was asleep, though, he sought Penny out. 'It is time we talked.' There was grimness both in his voice and in the set of his mouth. And when he looked at her Penny shivered all over. It was hard to imagine that they'd made this baby together, that their bodies had become one and she'd felt special.

'There's not much to say.' Penny made an effort to meet his eyes. They were dark and forbidding, with nothing at all like the soft sensuality she had seen when he was making love. 'I did a home test today—it proved positive.' As far as she was concerned it was evidence enough.

Very faintly he nodded. 'In that case, if it is true, then we have arrangements to make.'

'Such as?' queried Penny, conscious that her voice had risen sharply, even though she wanted to remain calm. 'If you're going to ask me again to marry you, forget it. It's out of the question.'

'Because?' he snapped.

'Because we don't love each other,' she returned equally sharply. 'Because we wouldn't be happy together. You're a workaholic, while I believe a man should make time for his family. There are infinite reasons. I won't deny you access but I'm definitely bringing this child up on my own. And I'm quitting my job.'

'What if I say you're a liar?'

Penny frowned. 'On which count? I am pregnant. I am giving up this job. I am bringing this child up on my own.'

'But you're lying when you say you don't love me.'

Her heart did a swift shuffle and her throat jammed. She tried to swallow but nothing happened. He was trying to sweep her into a corner from which there was no escape. Not for his sake, but for the children's. He wanted her to continue looking after Chloe, and ultimately this baby who had been conceived of their passion. He couldn't cope on his own and he'd found no other suitable person.

'Love you?' she echoed, hearing the wild fear in her

voice. 'I've enjoyed having sex with you, Santo. But I have no intention of falling in love ever again.'

She heard rather than saw the harsh breath he drew, but she did observe the thinning of his lips and the way his eyelids lowered over his eyes until they were almost but not quite closed. 'And that's all it was, sex? I've had sex with women before, and it was nothing like what you and I experienced.'

'What are you saying?' Penny lifted her chin and eyed him coolly, hoping he would believe that his words didn't bother her. He was making it sound as though the whole experience had meant a lot more to him than she'd suspected. And if that was the case...

'I think that you've fallen in love with me. I think you're running scared. I think you believe that I'm like Max and will drop you like a red-hot coal when I find someone better. But how could that be, when I've found the woman I want to spend the rest of my life with?'

Penny's blue eyes widened dramatically, turning into huge, wide, disbelieving orbs. She shook her head, unable to believe what he was saying.

'You think I'm not telling the truth? Why would I lie about something so important?' He took a step closer, close enough for her to feel the warmth of his body, his fresh breath on her face. 'I'm asking you again, Penny; will you marry me?'

'You actually mean it?'

'*Mio dio*, what does it take to convince you?'

'But—but you don't love me. You're doing this for the baby's sake. I could never marry you for that reason.'

'Do you love me?'

Penny didn't answer. How could she, when he'd never actually said that he loved her?

'Perhaps this will persuade you.' Without warning he took her face between his palms and kissed her, deeply and satisfyingly, and it wasn't long before Penny returned his kisses, urging her body closer, exulting in his hardness, and the fleeting thought passed through her mind that marrying Santo might very well be worth the risk.

Perhaps in time he would learn to love her as she loved him. Could she do it? Dared she do it?

He eased his lips away from hers, gentle fingers tracing her eyebrows, the line of her nose, the curve of her ears. 'There was only one reason I went to see my father.'

Penny couldn't see what this had to do with him suggesting they get married, nevertheless she waited patiently for him to continue.

'I wanted to introduce you as the woman I intended marrying. As my fiancée.'

Penny's mouth fell open. 'You did?'

'I thought he might have changed. I thought he might be pleased for me. But no, his behaviour was as appalling as it's ever been. I couldn't do it. I couldn't force him on you like that. There's no saying how he would have taken it, what he would have said. He could have hurt you so much.'

'You were going to declare that I was your fiancée without even asking whether I wanted to marry you?' Penny's thoughts ran riot. He'd had this in his mind all the time. He'd braved his father for her sake—Chloe's as well—but he'd actually been going to tell Antonio that he'd found the love of his life and planned to marry her.

And Antonio had ruined it…

No wonder he'd been in such a foul mood. No wonder he'd never spoken to his father unless it was absolutely necessary.

'I knew you'd agree to marry me,' he said with a wide smile that revealed his beautiful, even teeth. 'You love me, Penny. Go on, deny it. Tell me you don't and I'll let you walk away.'

'Oh, Santo...' Such happiness as she had never felt before swept over her, filled her, warmed her. Tears welled at the thought that this man, whom she had been going to desert, loved her enough to face his hostile parent. He'd wanted to tell him that this was the woman he loved; he'd wanted to show her off.

Instead his father's welcome had been hostile. It was only to Chloe and herself that he'd shown any warmth, and perhaps that hadn't been genuine. 'I really had hoped that you and your father would make up,' she said.

'I'd hoped so too, for your sake and for Chloe's. But since it's not to be let's forget him and concentrate solely on us. Do you love me enough to marry me? Or do you need a little more persuasion?'

'Maybe a little,' she answered with a mischievous smile.

His kiss melted her soul. She clung to him as though she never wanted to let him go, as though she was afraid that this moment wasn't real, that it was all a dream and she would wake to find that Santo didn't want her after all.

But he was still there, smiling down at her, his eyes full of love and tenderness and a promise of things to come. 'So it's a yes, then?'

'With one proviso.'

'Anything for you, *cara*. Anything.' It was spoken from the heart.

'I don't want a workaholic husband whom I never see. I want you to delegate, hand the reins over to someone else. Isn't your home life more important?'

'It never has been,' he said with a wry twist of his lips. 'I guess it's a throwback to the years spent under my father's thumb. I needed to escape. And work was the only way out. But for you, *il mio tesoro*, anything. You have no idea how often I've wanted to race home to you. I was afraid of scaring you away, though, I wanted you so much.'

'As I wanted you, my darling,' she breathed against his lips.

'I love you, Penny. I never thought I'd fall in love again. You're a very special person.'

'And I love you too, Santo. I will love you for the rest of my life. I promise you that.'

Penny and Santo got married almost immediately. Chloe was their bridesmaid and she was as proud as punch when they presented her with a baby brother seven months later.

'We must take him to see my Italian grandfather,' she declared importantly.

Penny and Santo looked at each other and because they were both feeling sentimental Santo nodded. 'One day, my little love, we will. We'll visit him again.'

Penny smiled inwardly. She hoped they did. She hoped that Santo would make one further attempt to heal the rift between him and his father. The man wasn't getting any younger. Nor would it be right for him to die before he'd seen his new grandchild.

Later that year they made the visit. By this time

Penny was pregnant again and they'd debated whether to wait until the baby was born, but Vittorio had phoned to say Antonio was ill.

They made it just in time. Penny's lasting impression was of father and son holding hands. Chloe kissed her grandfather and introduced her little brother before Penny ushered them out of the room.

When Santo came to find her he had tears in his eyes. 'At least we made our peace.'

Penny nodded. 'I'm proud of you, Santo. And I love you so very, very much.'

'As I love you, my darling, with all of my heart. For always.'

* * * * *

*Harlequin offers a romance for every mood!
See below for a sneak peek from our
paranormal romance line, Silhouette® Nocturne™.
Enjoy a preview of REUNION by USA TODAY
bestselling author Lindsay McKenna.*

Aella closed her eyes and sensed a distinct shift, like movement from the world around her to the unseen world.

She opened her eyes. And had a slight shock at the man standing ten feet away. He wasn't just any man. Her heart leaped and pounded. He reminded her of a fierce warrior from an ancient civilization. Incan? She wasn't sure but she felt his deep power and masculinity.

I'm Aella. Are you the guardian of this sacred site? she asked, hoping her telepathy was strong.

Fox's entire body soared with joy. Fox struggled to put his personal pleasure aside.

Greetings, Aella. I'm the assistant guardian to this sacred area. You may call me Fox. How can I be of service to you, Aella? he asked.

I'm searching for a green sphere. A legend says that the Emperor Pachacuti had seven emerald spheres created for the Emerald Key necklace. He had seven of his priestesses and priests travel the world to hide these spheres from evil forces. It is said that when all seven spheres are found, restrung and worn, that Light will return to the Earth. The fourth sphere is here, at your sacred site. Are you aware of it? Aella held her breath. She loved looking at him, especially his sensual mouth. The desire to kiss him came out of nowhere.

Fox was stunned by the request. *I know of the Emerald Key necklace because I served the emperor at the time it was created. However, I did not realize that one of the spheres is here.*

Aella felt sad. Why? Every time she looked at Fox, her heart felt as if it would tear out of her chest. *May I stay in touch with you as I work with this site?* she asked.

Of course. Fox wanted nothing more than to be here with her. To absorb her ephemeral beauty and hear her speak once more.

Aella's spirit lifted. What *was* this strange connection between them? Her curiosity was strong, but she had more pressing matters. In the next few days, Aella knew her life would change forever. How, she had no idea....

Look for REUNION
by USA TODAY *bestselling author*
Lindsay McKenna,
available April 2010, only from
Silhouette® Nocturne™.

Silhouette *Desire*

OLIVIA GATES

BILLIONAIRE, M.D.

Dr. Rodrigo Valderrama has it all...
everything but the woman he's secretly
desired and despised. A woman forbidden
to him—his brother's widow.
And she's pregnant.

Cybele was injured in a plane crash
and lost her memory. All she knows is
she's falling for the doctor who has swept her
away to his estate to heal. If only the secrets
in his eyes didn't promise to tear
them forever apart.

Available March wherever you buy books.

Always Powerful, Passionate and Provocative.

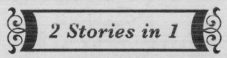

HER MEDITERRANEAN PLAYBOY

Sexy and dangerous—he wants you in his bed!

The sky is blue, the azure sea is crashing
against the golden sand and the sun is hot.

The conditions are perfect for
a scorching Mediterranean seduction
from two irresistible untamed playboys!

Indulge your senses with these two delicious stories

A MISTRESS AT THE ITALIAN'S COMMAND
by Melanie Milburne

ITALIAN BOSS, HOUSEKEEPER MISTRESS
by Kate Hewitt

Available April 2010 from Harlequin Presents!

www.eHarlequin.com

HP12910

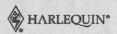

INTRIGUE

WILL THIS REUNITED FAMILY
BE STRONG ENOUGH TO EXPOSE
A LURKING KILLER?

FIND OUT IN THIS ALL-NEW
THRILLING TRILOGY FROM TOP
HARLEQUIN INTRIGUE AUTHOR

B.J. DANIELS

WHITEHORSE
MONTANA

Winchester Ranch

GUN-SHY BRIDE—*April 2010*

HITCHED—*May 2010*

TWELVE-GAUGE GUARDIAN—
June 2010

LARGER-PRINT BOOKS!

HARLEQUIN *Presents*~

GET 2 FREE LARGER-PRINT NOVELS PLUS 2 FREE GIFTS!

YES! Please send me 2 FREE LARGER-PRINT Harlequin Presents® novels and my 2 FREE gifts (gifts are worth about $10). After receiving them, if I don't wish to receive any more books, I can return the shipping statement marked "cancel". If I don't cancel, I will receive 6 brand-new novels every month and be billed just $4.55 per book in the U.S. or $5.24 per book in Canada. That's a saving of 13% off the cover price! It's quite a bargain! Shipping and handling is just 50¢ per book in the U.S. and 75¢ per book in Canada.* I understand that accepting the 2 free books and gifts places me under no obligation to buy anything. I can always return a shipment and cancel at any time. Even if I never buy another book, the two free books and gifts are mine to keep forever.

176 HDN E4GC   376 HDN E4GN

Name _____ (PLEASE PRINT)

Address _____ Apt. #

City _____ State/Prov. _____ Zip/Postal Code

Signature (if under 18, a parent or guardian must sign)

Mail to the Harlequin Reader Service:
IN U.S.A.: P.O. Box 1867, Buffalo, NY 14240-1867
IN CANADA: P.O. Box 609, Fort Erie, Ontario L2A 5X3

Not valid for current subscribers to Harlequin Presents Larger-Print books.

**Are you a subscriber to Harlequin Presents books and want to receive the larger-print edition?
Call 1-800-873-8635 today!**

* Terms and prices subject to change without notice. Prices do not include applicable taxes. Sales tax applicable in N.Y. Canadian residents will be charged applicable provincial taxes and GST. Offer not valid in Quebec. This offer is limited to one order per household. All orders subject to approval. Credit or debit balances in a customer's account(s) may be offset by any other outstanding balance owed by or to the customer. Please allow 4 to 6 weeks for delivery. Offer available while quantities last.

Your Privacy: Harlequin Books is committed to protecting your privacy. Our Privacy Policy is available online at www.eHarlequin.com or upon request from the Reader Service. From time to time we make our lists of customers available to reputable third parties who may have a product or service of interest to you. If you would prefer we not share your name and address, please check here. ☐

Help us get it right—We strive for accurate, respectful and relevant communications. To clarify or modify your communication preferences, visit us at www.ReaderService.com/consumerschoice.

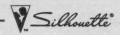

SPECIAL EDITION

**INTRODUCING A BRAND-NEW MINISERIES
FROM *USA TODAY* BESTSELLING AUTHOR**

KASEY MICHAELS

SECOND-CHANCE
BRIDAL

At twenty-eight, widowed single mother
Elizabeth Carstairs thinks she's left love behind
forever....until she meets Will Hollingsbrook.
Her sons' new baseball coach is the handsomest
man she's ever seen—and the more time they
spend together, the more undeniable the
connection between them. But can Elizabeth
leave the past behind and open her heart to
a second chance at love?

FIND OUT IN

SUDDENLY A BRIDE

*Available in April
wherever books are sold.*

HARLEQUIN Presents

EXTRA

**Presents Extra brings you
two new exciting collections!**

REGALLY WED

For the prince's bed

Rich, Ruthless and Secretly Royal #97
by ROBYN DONALD

Forgotten Mistress, Secret Love-Child #98
by ANNIE WEST

RUTHLESS TYCOONS

Powerful, merciless and in control!

Taken by the Pirate Tycoon #99
by DAPHNE CLAIR

Italian Marriage: In Name Only #100
by KATHRYN ROSS

*Available April 2010
from Harlequin Presents EXTRA!*